Unicorn

YOUR

LIFE

STERLING
New York

An Imprint of Sterling Publishing Co., Inc.
1166 Avenue of the Americas
New York, NY 10036

© 2018 Tandem Books, Inc.

ISBN 978-1-4549-3020-4

Distributed in Canada by Sterling Publishing Co., Inc.
c/o Canadian Manda Group, 664 Annette Street
Toronto, Ontario, Canada M6S 2C8
Distributed in the United Kingdom by GMC Distribution Services
Castle Place, 166 High Street, Lewes, East Sussex, England BN7 1XU
Distributed in Australia by NewSouth Books
45 Beach Street, Coogee, NSW 2034, Australia

For information about custom editions, special sales, and premium
and corporate purchases, please contact Sterling Special Sales
at 800-805-5489 or specialsales@sterlingpublishing.com.

Manufactured in China

2 4 6 8 10 9 7 5 3 1

sterlingpublishing.com

Design by Ashley Prine, Tandem Books
Illustrations by Drue Wagner
Holographic pattern on cover and title page by mything/Shutterstock.com
Ray background pattern throughout by Sira Anamwong/Shutterstock.com

Unicorn
YOUR
LIFE

Wondrous Ways
to Make Everything
MORE MAGICAL

MARY FLANNERY

ILLUSTRATIONS BY DRUE WAGNER

STERLING
New York

"WELL, NOW THAT WE HAVE SEEN EACH OTHER," SAID THE UNICORN, "IF YOU'LL BELIEVE IN ME, I'LL BELIEVE IN YOU."

– *THROUGH THE LOOKING-GLASS* BY LEWIS CARROLL

CONTENTS

INTRODUCTION

RIGHT NOW, SOMEWHERE IN THE world, there is a quiet cave full of gorgeous, glittering crystals. Somewhere else, in a desert, there is a tall cactus with a single flower at the top, blossoming in the hot sun. Still elsewhere there is a bakery making delicate, delicious pastel macarons; a girl braiding her vibrant rainbow hair; a school of iridescent fish darting below a bridge of pink coral; a fairy cozying up on the couch in one of those backward robes that everyone thought was a cool new blanket invention. OK, that last one may or may not be real, but the world is full of magic. In fact, it *is* magic! And to be a unicorn within it, all you need to do is see that magic all around you.

There is wonder and laughter to be found in every part of your life if you just turn your horn to it. If you keep an eye peeled for all that sparkles and is kind, instead of all that molders and is mean, you'll see so much more cool stuff everywhere. With a glittery outlook, you'll fill up your brain and hear with awesome instead of awful. So muck that negative junk—you're a dazzling creation of magical amazingness!

Unicorns are symbols of this philosophy. They are horses, gorgeous creatures in themselves, with a little extra twist of enchantment: a horn that turns an ordinary animal into a wondrous beast. They are that magic you can find in yourself and the world around you if you look for gold and refuse to revel in refuse. They represent the act of turning mundane moments into cotton-candy extravaganzas.

Unicorn Your Life is your guide not only to spotting all that sparkles but also to making magic of your own. It's not about pretending that bad things don't exist but about focusing on the good and being generous toward yourself and others. It's also about rainbows and glitter! *Sooooo much glitter!!!*

Unicorning your life is like this: Think about something that is simple and common but also so wonderful it makes you smile and shimmy with delight. Maybe it's an achingly adorable puppy, a sunset streaked with pinks and purples, your favorite candy, or squishy toy caticorn (cat + unicorn) that smells like strawberries. That little fluttering warmth you feel when you revel in a simple pleasure, when you're tickled by kitten whiskers, when you inhale the amazing artificial sweetness of an off-gassing toy so hard that your head spins a little, *that's* a unicorn moment! And you don't have to chance upon those moments like a maiden finding a fairy in the forest. A real unicorn like you doesn't just sit on their pretty, pretty haunches waiting for happiness. You can actively

look for these moments, take them into your heart and hug them, and even make them yourself. If you do that, well, you're pretty much a magical unicorn—at least on the inside.

This book will take you through tons of ways you can unicorn your life. It starts with you and how awesome and wonderful and amazing you are. You'll uncover who your inner you(nicorn) truly is and how you can hold your horn high. Once you embrace your truly majestic self, you'll learn how to meditate like magic, see with unicorn vision, break bad old habits and form some dandy new ones, frolic with abandon, and, perhaps most importantly, give zero fudges about what all the ogres and trolls think.

Next, you'll unicorn your relationships by finding new ways to appreciate friends and family as well as special friends (wink wink, nudge nudge). By meeting others on their own terms and truly seeing them for who they are, your expectations of them can fall away so that you can love them with a pure, golden unicorn heart. Also, dance parties!

Then, it's time for unicorning your home—making your abode into a magical place where you are happy and at ease in its cushy adorableness. Creating special spots where you can recharge your sense of sparkly wonder, probably while eating candy, is essential to the unicorn philosophy.

Finally, once you're fortified with all sorts of wonderful unicorniness, you can unicorn your job. This is, for many unicorns, a decidedly unmagical part of their otherwise pearly existence. But that doesn't mean you can't find rainbows and charm at work. Find out how to deal with credit vampires, office ogres, and beastly bosses with the grace and poise of a unicorn, as well as make some magic that will get you through your days with higher spirits.

In *Unicorn Your Life* you'll discover all sorts of ways to make squee-worthy cuteness, heart-warming enchantment, and glittery goodness the biggest and best parts of your life. Some are as easy as identifying what makes you feel good and creating more time for that. Others require a bit more brain work. It's easy to get sucked down into the muck of negativity when things go wrong or the world seems chaotic. But with practice, glitter, persistence, glitter, true love, glitter, and a happy heart and horn, you really can make your life—or at least a lot of it—into a fairy tale.

A CREATURE GUIDE

A number of creatures who wish they were as cool as unicorns are mentioned throughout these pages. Here is a quick guide to each of them.

Demons Friggen jerks.

Elves These cool creatures are smart, sexy (Arwen and Legolas, I'm looking at you!), and make great unicorn companions.

Fairies These super-fun creatures are great at parties and have an absolutely adorbs sense of style. Their souls are made of squee.

Giants These big cheeses are powerful beasts that aren't necessarily good or evil, but they are all business.

Gnomes They may look like elves but they act like goblins. Every last one of them has the middle name Negative Nancy.

Goblins Nasty pieces of work who are always judging you and your work. Blech!

Imps Easily irritated, imps are always creating mischief to vent some of their frustration at always being irritated. It's a vicious magic circle.

Leprechauns OMG! So cute and fun and *rich*!

Manticores The dude equivalent of the sphinx who thinks he deserves more legroom than you do.

Minotaurs Really bull-headed creatures who are easily lost and usually enraged as a result.

Mummies Shambling ne'er-do-wells who are always groaning about other creatures.

Ogres and Trolls Cut from the same reeking cloth, these creatures are bullies who love throwing their weight around and despise all that's good and glittery.

Pegasi A close relative of the unicorn, pegasi are just like you but with wings instead of a horn, which sounds pretty rad.

Phoenixes Never count a phoenix out! They are resilient and fiery and badass.

Sphinxes Meow! These creatures are sexy as can be, but they're also kind of confusing, what with that lion head and lady body.

Vampires Your energy, your time, your ideas—anything that's yours, they want it! They'll suck you dry if you let them.

Witches and Warlocks Malevolent pains in the horn that take pleasure in messing with majestic creatures such as unicorns.

Yetis Big lunks that are sweet but also stinky.

UNICORN
YOU

THE FIRST STEP IN UNICORNING your life is to find, appreciate, love, squeeze, cherish, and glitterify that amazing unicorn inside you. How could you unicorn anything else if you haven't unicorned yourself? *But what does that even mean?* you may wonder. Unicorning may sound mystical, but really it's quite simple magic: you just need to close your eyes, take some deep breaths, and think about what makes you happy. What delights and enchants you and makes you want to frolic and sing and cavort and make all sorts of merry like some kind of mad, majestic merry-making machine?

Once you know what you love, you'll know what you want, and you'll know yourself—and then all you have to do is embrace that self. Squeeze yourself in a big happy hug and just frickin' love it! If it means wearing a sparkly tutu, *wear it*. If it means singing "I Will Survive" at the top of your lungs, *sing it*. Give yourself the tenderness and affection and respect and forgiveness and glittery gifts and freedom to be oneself that you would give your best friend and beloved. Loving your own horn (which is the core of you) is the best way to be happy, and by doing that, you'll find that love will work itself into all the nooks and crannies around you like so much spilled glitter. You just can't get rid of that stuff!

There are lots of ways you can get in touch with your inner you(nicorn), and this chapter goes over the most magical ones.

Journaling, meditating, visualization techniques, not giving a flying fudge about what others think, frolicking in a meadow, positive affirmations—these are all effective means of getting all up inside your own head and making merry. But like all forms of magic, these means of self-exploration can serve you well only if you believe they will.

You can make so much magic by *believing* you can make magic. You might not always succeed in accomplishing a thing you believe you can do, but you will almost never succeed in accomplishing a thing you don't think you can do. Believing that a thing will happen takes you an extraordinarily long way down the yellow brick road to it actually happening. There is only awesomeness to be gained by believing in yourself and your own amazing powers. There is only good to be had by thinking well of yourself. While going around bragging about yourself is just bravado—which is decidedly un-unicorn behavior—going around believing in yourself is just good sense.

YOU DO YOU(NICORN)

You are a sparkling, majestic creature, and I'm not just saying that! It's true. Everyone is a truly magical creation (granted, some tend toward the dark-magic variety), and the more you embrace who you are, the better you get. Sure, we all have flaws and foibles, bad habits we could break and evil warlocks we should really get around to vanquishing, but that essence of you—that spark in your core, that bit of magic that makes you a unique individual—is wondrous. It's also kind of a mysterious thing. What is that core bit? How do you know if you're being true to it? What the elf does it even mean to "be yourself"?!

It means really listening to that inner sage. That gut instinct. That voice beneath all the logic and reason and emotion and outsider advice and societal norms. That whisper of truth is in there, and when you follow it, confidence follows. Happiness follows. Things feel right. Your heart gleams a little extra. For instance, you spot a gauzy, shimmery toile tutu and are drawn to it like a mermaid to water. The grumpy gnome you're shopping with doesn't get it at all and tells you not to buy it, but you feel it: this tutu is you. So, you do you! Get the tutu! External forces and contemporary fashion mores be danged!

That's a super-fun but pretty superficial example. There are, of course, bigger concerns about what to do with your life, whom to love, where to live, what you feel driven to create, and how to send that evil warlock back to his own dimension. When it comes to that big stuff, there are so many factors screaming for your attention that they can drown out that whispering voice of true you. So when it comes to making big choices, just sit down and be quiet. Just think. Think about yourself and what you're doing. Think about what you *want* to be doing. Push out all the judgments from the world and from your own brain and really listen for that enchanting, whispering voice. Listen for honesty in it, and don't make excuses to ignore it. Because it's only when you do you, when you really learn who that you(nicorn) is, that you can find that kind of awesome bliss that comes from a magical life well lived.

SELF-CONFIDENCE FOR DAYS

Every mythical, magical, majestic beast is different, and that's what makes us all interesting and marvelous. (It also makes some of us, well, stinky. I'm looking at you, yetis!) But just because everyone has their own brand of magic, that doesn't mean there aren't a lot of trolls out there trying to bring you down. Judgy goblins, undercutting mummies, intimidating ogres—there are lots of foul beasts out there, and that's not even counting your own inner demons of self-deprecation and uncertainty. You just have to tune out all those monsters and focus on all your many, many, many, many positive points. Those are the keys to the self-confidence kingdom!

As with so many things, self-confidence comes from the stories you tell yourself. If you keep repeating horror stories about all the times you slipped up, did something embarrassing, or had some idiotic ogre insult you, you'll think that's who you really are. It's so easy to fall into this trap in times of stress, on nights when you can't sleep, or really any ol' time. But if you instead tell yourself tales of triumph and awesomeness, friendship and love, then that's the you that you will come to identify with. The next time you catch yourself going down a dark memory lane, switch paths. Call up a good memory instead, and focus in on it. This can be some hard mental work, but the more and more you bring your brain back

to the positive, the easier it will be to get there and stay there. And all self-confidence is, after all, is thinking nice thoughts about yourself!

NICE TAIL! BODY POSITIVITY FOR ALL

There are as many shapes and sizes as there are creatures in the world. No two bodies are exactly the same—no, not even identical twins, smarty-horn—and that's awesome! But even though there is beautiful variety all around us all the time, it often feels like there are only a few acceptable shapes and sizes. That's because we see so much in the media (TV, movies, magazines, online stores, the Internet generally, catalogs) that shows us the same kinds of creatures all the time, and while those we see are often beautiful, they are just a very small sliver of what beauty looks like. What we see the most conditions us to what we think we *should* see, and so when we look in the mirror, which does not come with a Photoshop option, we often feel like we don't measure up. We focus on every lump, bump, pimple, and pudge.

But that's Pegasus plop! When you look in that mirror, pick out the things you like instead and focus on those. Start by imagining you're not even looking at you. Pretend you're looking at a friend you adore, and only tell yourself the things you'd say to someone you really love and admire. Because you, of all unicorns, deserve your own love and admiration. You work so hard for yourself all the time! Be at least as generous with yourself as you would be with your best friend.

Also, look at yourself often. Not in that microanalyzing way in which you spot every hair out of place and agonize over how big your eyes are, nor in a vainglorious way, but in the way in which you catch a lot of glimpses of yourself so you look normal to yourself. You get used to you. Lots of people who have come to love their bodies swear by this process, whereby they get used to what they look like and then come to love it.

You can also seek out images of lots of creatures, big and small, and get used to looking at them. Creature-watch in public and be kind in your opinions. If you stop judging others, it can go a long way toward helping you stop judging yourself. Admire their lustrous coats, strong limbs, unique features, and radiant selves. Get happy with lots of body types, but while you're doing it, resist the urge to compare you(nicorn) to them. They aren't you, and you aren't them, but you're all beautilicious!

All of this may sound like magic to you. You may feel like body positivity is on a high golden mountaintop and you're stuck in a deep, dark forest. You might not even believe you're worthy of getting out of the forest, never mind climbing the mountain. And you'd be right in that it is a kind of magic, but it's a magic mind trick that you can do. Beauty is literally in the eye of the beholder, and you are that beholder. You have the power to change your mind. It's not always easy, and it certainly doesn't happen in a twinkly flash. It takes time and dedication. But if you're not worth the effort, what is?!

FINDING GOLDEN LININGS

The expression "silver lining" comes from the 1634 work *Comus* by John Milton:

> *Was I deceived? or did a sable cloud*
> *Turn forth her silver lining on the night?*
> *I did not err; there does a sable cloud,*
> *Turn forth her silver lining on the night*
> *And casts a gleam over this tufted grove.*

Who knew it was such an old saying?! Well, nerds did, I suppose. Anyhoo, the idea that a dark cloud has a silvery lunar lining is certainly charming, and the proverb has endured for centuries, but why settle for a second-place lining from the moon when you can have a golden lining from the sun?

You can spot a golden lining in any situation with a little imagination. Every obstacle is a learning experience; every ogre you have to endure shows you how awesome it is to be you instead of being said ogre; and even a tragedy can have the benefit of bringing people together. It's important to remember that finding the golden lining does not negate the cloud. It doesn't make it disappear, discount it, or make it unimportant. Some dark clouds warrant solemnity and deference, but it does them no disrespect to try to find some good around them. And looking for those positive rays of sun will help make dark days easier to bear.

AFFIRMATIONS THAT SPARKLE

Magic is made by the stories you tell yourself. A good story makes for a good time, a good impression, a good point of view. Affirmations are little gold nuggets of positivity that you can repeat in your head or out loud to reinforce the attitude you want to have about, well, anything. Your day, your life, your job, your body, your sparkling personality, your friends, your family. You can attach an affirmation to anything you want to feel good about to help you get there. They are also great for shooing away dark thoughts; anytime dark clouds gather in your mind, a good affirmation can blow those thunderheads away and bring on the sun.

Here are some gems for you to peruse and use. Feel free to make up your own, too—just make sure they're short and sweet and make you feel neat!

I make my own magic!

I am beautiful!

I am powerful!

I am super talented!

I am full of forgiveness!

I am a magical elfing unicorn!

Everyone is on their own path, and I'm only in charge of my own!

Every day I love [name a family, friend, or loved one] more and more!

I will love myself even more
today than I did yesterday!

I am a creative force!

I have accomplished so
much, and I've barely
even started!

I choose happiness! I choose
magic! I choose love!

Only I can tell me what to do!

I run this show!

My friends are the coolest!

Life is full of changes, and I
love the excitement!

My future is going to rock,
and it starts today!

I am one smooth operator!

Today is another day when
I'll sparkle and shine!

I trample obstacles!

There isn't anything I
can't do!

Make money, make money,
make money!

Life is beautiful!

Happiness is worth
working for!

This BS is only temporary!

Give love, make love,
take love!

The world is magical!

I am so proud of my (name
accomplishment or point
of pride)!

If I dream it, I can do it!

I've got what it takes!

TREAT YOURSELF

There is nothing like a little self-care to refresh and recharge your sparkle. Taking the time to pamper yourself is so super important for maintaining a positive outlook, an energetic attitude, and a lustrous horn. It's officially now on your must-do priority list, right up there with eating, sleeping, and pooping rainbows.

Treating yourself can take any form you want it to, as long as it tickles you and makes you feel that shoulder-shimmying glee that comes from pure indulgence. Here is a list of treats you can, and should, give yourself:

- ♥ get a massage
- ♥ eat your favorite meal
- ♥ go shopping
- ♥ binge-watch your favorite movie trilogy
- ♥ reread your favorite book
- ♥ get a sparkly, glittery, glorious manicure
- ♥ pet some puppies
- ♥ cuddle some kittens
- ♥ buy or pick yourself some flowers
- ♥ bake a Rainbow Cake (see page 175)
- ♥ go in a sensory-deprivation tank
- ♥ go to the spa

- ♥ go poolside
- ♥ go beachside
- ♥ take a nap
- ♥ aromatherapy up your home
- ♥ meditate
- ♥ make art
- ♥ go hiking
- ♥ get the comfiest socks you can find
- ♥ take a long soak in the tub
- ♥ CANDY!!!
- ♥ share a really good bottle of wine with a really good friend
- ♥ get some decadent lotion
- ♥ take a relaxing yoga class
- ♥ doodle with reckless abandon
- ♥ dance party!
- ♥ catch a sunrise or sunset
- ♥ go for a stroll
- ♥ check out a museum
- ♥ wear your favorite outfit
- ♥ find a fun Pinterest craft and do it
- ♥ call someone you love and talk for hours
- ♥ give yourself an entire day off from computer, phone, and TV screens

MEDITATION IS MAGIC

Meditation is mind magic that makes your life better. Like all awesome things, it takes some work and isn't necessarily easy, but its wondrousness is more than worth it. People who make meditation part of their routine have reduced stress levels (awesome), better concentration (yes, please!), better emotional control and evenness (ahhhhh). They also age more slowly (seriously? seriously!) and are just all around happier (magic!).[1]

It's a common misconception that to meditate you have to be some great guru or serious sage, but that's just trollshit. Meditation is all about taking it easy, letting go, and just being. Don't get all hung up on how to do it, or whether you're doing it wrong, or anything like that. Just do it, and you're doing it. It really is that easy!

All you need to start is two minutes in the morning. Just two little minutes before you enter the pantheon of your day. Sit down comfortably—no need to force yourself into any fancy positions that make your feet fall asleep. Just sit and chill. Use pillows if that makes you comfier. Close your eyes and check in with yourself. How are you doing? How are you feeling? Whatever the answer, that's OK; just check in to see how your horn is hanging.

Then breathe. *Just breathe.* Bring all your attention to taking air in through your nose, deep into your lungs, and out

through your mouth. Your thoughts will wander, and that's fine. Just bring them back to your breathing as soon as you notice them scampering away. If they're really running wild, count your breaths: one in, two out, three in, four out, and so on. Some people get hung up on the idea that meditation means clearing your mind completely, but that ain't gonna happen. Or at least it's not likely, especially at first, and it's definitely not the goal. There is no thought—or lack thereof—that is the goal. All you're doing is giving yourself a chance to *just be*. When you're done, smile and thank yourself for giving yourself the gift of awesome.

After you've been doing two minutes of meditation every morning for a few days, a week, or however long it takes you to feel like you could comfortably add more time to your meditation routine, then do just that. If you need a little help, there are lots of apps and videos out there that can guide you through meditation and are great for getting you started, keeping you on course, and introducing you to more advanced techniques.

UNICORN VISION

Another way to hone and use your mental unicorn powers is through visualization exercises, which when you're unicorning your life are known as *unicorn vision.* It is a bit like meditating, in that you sit comfortably with your eyes closed and start by focusing on your breathing. But instead of passively allowing yourself to be, you actively pursue a super-majestically magical mental scenario that can help you beat stress, manage pain, amp you up, conquer fears, or get the gold—gold being pretty much anything you want it to be, including visualizing stealing a pot of gold from a leprechaun (no judgments!).

Visualization exercises work by getting your brain totally on board with your wants. For instance, public speaking may give you the creepies and make you want to run screaming. But if you get used to picturing yourself being frickin' awesome at speaking to crowds, then when you go to do it for real, your ol' flight instinct won't get triggered.

On top of that, thinking that something is going to happen really does increase the chances of it actually happening. If you want to be a famous artist, but you don't think it will ever happen and have no plan to make it happen, it most certainly won't happen! But if you think, *I'm going to do this!* and imagine yourself doing it, make a plan to do it, and follow that plan, the chances are immensely greater than zero that you will do it.

Research even shows that athletes who envision their bodies doing spectacular things are more likely to do spectacular things![2]

Here is a basic unicorn-vision exercise to get you started.

THE HAPPY RAINBOW

You are a unicorn. You are resting in a peaceful field. The sun is warm as it shines down on you, glinting off your golden horn. The grass is tickling your belly where you lie. Flowers bob in a cool breeze that carries their sweet smell to your nose and rustles your rainbow mane. You hear the distant buzz of friendly bumblebees. A beautiful, bright rainbow rises from the horizon. It arcs across the sky and shines down right on you, full of radiant happiness that travels slowly through you. It beams down into your horn, energizing your mind. You breathe it in, filling your lungs with its calm joy. It shines in your heart, making it beat strong and steady. It glows in your belly and radiates through your sturdy legs. You absorb the happiness of the rainbow and become full of its magical charm so that there is no room left inside you for anything other than delight and contentment.

TAKE MINI MIND VACATIONS TO YOUR HAPPY PLACE

A really fun and relaxing unicorn-vision exercise is to build your very own imaginary happy place and then take mini mind vacations there whenever you're feeling stressed, low energy, or just bleh. The sparkling, starry sky isn't even the limit when it comes to your happy place: it can be in space, underwater, inside a rainbow, on top of a cloud, or literally anywhere else you can imagine.

There's no rush to build your happy place. You can start by just picking a setting and visualizing yourself there. Then, each time you go, build another cool element. It could be a waterfall of pure happiness that washes away all your negativity and fills you with joy when you walk through it. It could be a beam of healing energy that eases your pain, or a cupboard full of elixirs of strength to make you super swole. It could be a glittery tornado that covers you with tiny diamonds and leaves a trail of playful kittens as it blows past.

You can make your happy place anything you like and take mini mind vacations there as often as you want. The more you visit it, the better it will be. And the more you follow the same path to get there each time, meaning you envision the same things whenever you embark on your vacation, the stronger the vision will be and the easier it will be to get there.

ENCHANTING CHAKRAS

According to the ancient Indian Vedic texts, chakras are the places in the body where we hold different kinds of energy. They're where the mojo flows! The word itself roughly means "wheel" or disk" in Sanskrit, and each chakra has a color associated with it, so you can picture your body as a rainbow of powerful orbs running from the base of your spine to the top of your head. When we feel good, that means our energy is flowing freely through our chakra highway. If we are feeling bad, a chakra might be jammed up like rush-hour traffic before a holiday weekend. Eating well and practicing yoga generally keep our chakras open and energetic, but each one can be individually balanced through techniques like the following and by envisioning that chakra's color.

Root Chakra Red and located at the base of your spine. It fuels our survival instincts and makes us feel secure. To keep it happy, you need to get your blood pumping with exercises like dancing, jumping, or running.

Sacral Chakra Orange and located in your lower abdomen. It energizes our desire for pleasure, creativity, and sexuality. Hip-opening stretches are great for keeping sacral balance.

Solar Plexus Chakra Yellow and located in your tummy. It is all about power and manifesting your destiny; it's your smarts and your will. It's where your fire is! It's one of the easiest chakras to block up, but you can balance it through meditation, aromatherapy, and yoga's warrior pose.

Heart Chakra Green and located in the center of your chest. It is home to love, compassion, and relationships. Having it free flowing and balanced will help you relate to others and maintain healthy relationships. Meditation and positive affirmations are great for your heart chakra.

Throat Chakra Blue and located exactly where you think it is. It is where your speech and truth lie, along with your self-expression and all your communication. To help stay loud and proud, drink plenty of water, sing a song, and wear a blue necklace.

Third-Eye Chakra Indigo and located in the center of your forehead where your horn is. It is where your awareness, your intuition, and your insight live. It is your guiding light. Meditation and unicorn vision will keep it wide open and all seeing.

Crown Chakra A brilliant violet color and located at the top of your head. It is where spirituality, consciousness, and your connection to the universe live. Meditation, peace and quiet, and slow stretching and breathing are great for keeping your crown on your head.

TECH IS AND IS NOT MAGIC

Having the entire universe of information and connectivity at your hooftips is amazing, astounding, and kind of magical. Mostly. Sort of. A bit. There is practically nothing you can't know with just a few taps on a screen. That's incredible! But of course, when there is something so good and powerful, there's always a dark force to counterbalance it. The bright, flashing screens we live with are really great at giving us little reward bursts. Likes, thumbs-ups, candies getting crushed, binging and pinging, messages coming in—they are all tiny prizes that set off the feel-good brain magic of dopamine. This is wonderful for quick bursts of pleasure. The kicker, though, is that the more dopamine you get, the more of it you need to feel the same amount of happy. That's why so many of our fellow creatures look like their phones are glued to their paws. What's worse is that too much dopamine (we all have and need certain amounts of it) drowns out another even more magical brain chemical, serotonin.

Serotonin is responsible for making you feel a lasting sense of happiness and contentment, and a lack of it causes depression. The cruel hands of fate have fashioned us in such a way that the more we succumb to little impulses for pleasure, the harder it is for us to manufacture the richer, long-lasting feel-goods. Limiting screen time is so hard because the likes and pings are literally addictive: they're giving you dopamine to send you a jolt of pleasure and then upping your need for dopamine to get to the same happy place, all while burying the real happy deeper and deeper. Booooo! This sucks! And it's a hard cycle to get out of. Lucky for you, you're a powerful unicorn who can beat the siren song of screen addiction.[3]

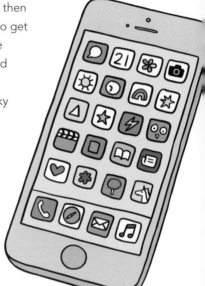

Here are some amazing things you can do that involve no screens and actually up your serotonin production:

- 💗 get out in that amazing sunshine— using sunscreen, of course
- 💗 get a massage—this seriously increases your serotonin production
- 💗 shake your groove thing—exercising and dancing are amazing for your bod and your brain
- 💗 take mini mind vacations (see page 37) and dwell on happy memories
- 💗 eat nutritious whole grain seeds such as quinoa and buckwheat

- ♡ get enough vitamin B6 from supplements or foods such as celery, garlic, fish, and spinach
- ♡ happy belly equals happy you(nicorn)—good digestion means good serotonin production, so get down with fermented foods and drinks like pickles, kimchi, and kombucha
- ♡ relax and meditate—a calm mind is a sparkly serotonin machine
- ♡ cut back on sugar—you may, cruelly, crave it when your serotonin is low, but that sweet substance produces dopamine like a tidal wave

TAKE IT LIKE A UNICORN: ON COMPLIMENTS

Compliments. They are meant to be kind. They are meant to make you feel good. They are meant to let you know that you rock and people know it. So why is it that they can make you feel so dang uncomfortable? We are not talking about "compliments" in the sense of catcalls from creepsters. We're talking about sincere compliments that are given by good people and come from a good place but still might make you squirm a little.

What is up with that?! Maybe you don't like the spotlight. Maybe deep down, you don't feel like you deserve the praise. Well, bollocks to that! You do deserve some complimentary high fives. And as for not liking a light being shone on you, even when it's on your gloriousness, well, learn to love it, my fine friend, and you'll do yourself a lot of good.

To realize your own awesomeness and take a compliment like a unicorn, do *not*:

- ♡ deflect it by putting it back on the complimenter (sure, they could be great, but we're talking about *you* right now!)
- ♡ think it is somehow disingenuous

♡ answer it by listing off your weaknesses

♡ attribute anything to luck

♡ say, "It was nothing" or "Anyone could have done it"

What you *do* do is:

♡ say thank you

♡ smile

♡ feel good!

That's it. Be as genuine as you can about it, and the more you do it, the better and more genuine it will actually feel. If you are so inclined, you can pay a compliment to the complimenter, so long as it's true and thoughtful and doesn't just put the compliment you received right back on them. You are not rubber, and they are not glue.

RAINBOW HEALING

Each color of the rainbow has its own energy, and color therapy uses these energies to heal different things. If you're into that sort of thing. You can do this by gazing at different colors (tapestries, painted walls, or other large blocks of color), or by shining colored lights at particular body parts or even your whole body. (Never stare directly into a light, no matter what color it is!)

Red is a super-energizing color! Shine a beam on achy joints to help soothe them or on limbs to energize them.

Orange really gets you going! It stimulates your heart and other organs. Shine a beam on your core to help energize your innards, but avoid shining it on your heart if you have high blood pressure.

Yellow is a wise color that can help your mental well-being by energizing your mind and clearing out any mental blocks. A beam of yellow light shone on the front of the neck is said to have particularly therapeutic effects.

Green is a very basic healing color, and it is a good idea to start and end a color-therapy session by bathing your whole body with a soothing light of true green (not too yellow or blue).

Blue is calming. You can shine it on the top of your head or the bottom of your feet to help nervousness and sleeplessness.

Violet light can be used over the whole body to bring a sense of contentment. Or it can be focused on the forehead (be careful not to shine it in your eyes!) for a similar effect.

BEGONE, BAD HABITS!

Everyone has a bad habit or two or twenty. Maybe you swear more often than is becoming of a unicorn. Maybe you oversleep, or you're always late, or you bite your hoofs. No matter what the thing is, anything that you don't want to do but somehow can't help yourself from doing is a bad habit. There are a few ways you can go about breaking the chains that bind you to any unwanted behavior; you just have to find which one (or which combination) works for you.

Be Aware of Your Triggers Figure out what makes you want to behave badly. Is it stress? Is it a time of day? Is it an ogre in your life? If you find out what makes you tick, then you can recognize when those triggers are happening and talk yourself out of responding to them. Awareness is a powerful thing.

Swap It Instead of acting on your impulse to do something you're compelled to but don't really want to do, take that moment to do something else and make a habit out of that. If you want to stop drinking soda, every time you crave that sweet elixir, have a club soda with a squeeze of lemon instead. If you want to wake up on time, swap hitting the snooze button for ringing a really loud but pretty bell. Consistency is key.

Unicorn Fact!

According to legend, you can only catch a unicorn by baiting it with a virgin. Not cool!

Sparkly, Sparkly Rewards and Dire Consequences Every time you successfully control your bad-habit impulse, give yourself a treat! A little nibble of chocolate, a quickie dance party, whatever you like. And every time you fail, fine yourself by putting a buck in a fail jar.

Get Out of There! If you want to ditch your bad habits, sometimes you have to get out of the patterns that make you want to be bad. If you shake up your routine and start doing new things, or doing things in a new order, you might not find yourself craving the same old bad stuff.

Twenty-Second Setback Whenever you get that bad-behavior feeling, count slowly to twenty while thinking about how much you want to break your habit. Often all you need is that moment of contemplating the gross, the ick, the hate you have for the habit to prevent you from giving in to your craving for it.

Think Your Way Out Focus really hard on how much you hate the thing you don't want to do. Come up with a visualization of how gross it is and how awful and nonmagical it makes you feel. Really get down and dirty with the ick of it. Exaggerate how bad it is in your mind and have that feeling ready, right on the tip of your brain, to call up anytime the urge to be bad hits.

MORE GLITTER!

Some people say there's such a thing as too much glitter, but they probably aren't unicorns. They might be fun fairies or eager elves, but they aren't *unicorns*. Unicorns can never have too much glitter, either literally or figuratively. Glitter makeup, glitter clothes, glitter hairspray, glitter shoes . . . well, you get the picture. Glitter is great! But metaphorical glitter is even better.

This is that little extra bit of magic you can put into something to really make it twinkle. You've got icing on the cake, but if you add some edible flowers, you've super upped the metaphorical glitter factor. Thinking of texting a friend to congratulate them on something? Plop on that! Write an actual letter and fill the envelope with confetti.

The soul of unicorning your life and glittering along the way is doing whatever you're doing with heart. It is recognizing how you can make something sparkle with just a little extra touch, a little bit more glitter, a little bit more love. Taking that extra magical step moves you from the everyday to the extraordinary day, and with only so many days to frolic on this earth, why not make each one as glittery as it can be?

GET IN HERE, GOOD HABITS!

Want to drink more water? Exercise more? Sleep more? Read more? Live, laugh, and love more? Making good behavior into a habit, a thing you do automatically without much thought or convincing, can be as much of a challenge as breaking a gnarly habit, but going through the effort is absolutely worth it. Why not make your life as rich and splendiferous as possible? Here are some great ways to get great at being great.

Begin Itty-Bitty If you try to revolutionize your life all at once, you'll definitely disappoint yourself. Instead, do something really tiny to start. If you want to eat healthier, start by adding one veg to each meal. If you want to read more, start with just a page a day. This way you won't intimidate yourself out of committing or exhaust your willpower.

Be Super Clear Having a vague idea about what you want to do doesn't cut it. If you want to exercise more, have an exact plan for what you ultimately want. Which days of the week? How long? What are your goals for weights lifted or weight off your body?

Celebrate Good Habits, Come On! Reward yourself when you succeed. If your goal is to drink more water and you managed to have a glass more in a day than you normally would, you win! Do something nice for yourself and tell yourself how happy you are. If you set up the reward pathway in your brain around your new habit, you'll soon love doing it.

BE A GIVE-A-CORN

Volunteering is kinda the best thing you can do. It gives to creatures in need, to your community, to the universe. It makes the world a sparklier place to be. Not only that, but you'll feel awesome about doing it. Self-esteem, self-worth, and self-awesome all skyrocket when you know you're spending your time well and lending a helping hoof.

Animal Shelters These are great places to volunteer. You get to pet kitties and walk doggies as you find them new homes and families. Love!

Food Pantries They can always use some extra help getting the word out about food drives or handing out supplies to folks in need.

National Parks They could sure use someone like you to help clean up litter, give tours of historic landmarks, and tend to the natural splendor.

Local Library Show these amazing places some love by volunteering to shelve books, assist lenders, and set up for events.

Habitat for Humanity Not only do you help out families in need, but you get to learn construction and home-maintenance skills! There's no expertise required.

Museums Big or small, they are always looking for art lovers to help with programs and activities.

Retirement Homes The residents and the staff would be psyched to have you come in and sing a little song, run a little bingo, or teach old folks to use computers. There are a ton of things you can do that are fun and will brighten lots of days.

JOURNALING FOR JOY

If you don't already keep a journal, go out and get the shimmeriest, most bedazzled, colorful rainbow diary of your dreams and *start*! Writing down your days, your thoughts, your dreams— anything and everything—is not only an amazing chronicle of your life but absolutely essential to getting to know yourself. Science even agrees that journaling is magic: studies have shown that journaling can up your emotional intelligence and help you process your emotions.[4] Better processing means less stress and more positivity. Journaling also helps you become more mindful. As you write down what's important in your days and in your mind, you'll be more cognizant of all that glitters in your life.

GOOOOOOOOOOAAAALLLS!!!

Journaling about your goals reinforces how important they are in your brain. The more you write about your goals, the more likely you are to score.

In addition, it'll make your memory better and help you understand your life. When you write, you have to think about what's going on and translate it into words. So where once you may have just had blurry feelings, journaling will give you crystal-clear ideas of what's up.

And finally, keeping a journal will help you heal when bad things happen. You go through all the bad stuff when you write it down, giving it a firm shape and getting it out of your head instead of letting a nebulous thought monster thrash around in your brain.

DON'T WORRY AND YOU REALLY WILL BE HAPPY

Worrying about stuff is really and truly pointless. You can mentally prepare for something. Carefully consider a situation. Even try to figure out the potential outcomes and what you should do for each of them—once. Not over and over again, catastrophizing bigger, uglier creative scenarios of fiery death and destruction each time. When you worry about something, turning it over and over in that fabulous mind of yours, not only will you suffer if your worries come true, but you've already suffered through them in your head countless times. And for what? The worrying gets you nothing. Hemming and hawing over hypotheticals is just a whole lot of pointlessness.

Of course, saying "Don't worry" and actually not worrying are two separate things, and the second falls into the easier-said-than-done category. It takes some work to get out of the worry rut, but it's work that's well worth it. When you start to worry, you have to switch tracks. If you're stressing about some troll giving you a hard time, whenever that worry pops into your head, think about pandas instead. Cute, cuddly pandas. Have you seen that video of all the baby pandas going down the slide and getting into a panda pileup at the bottom? Oh my god, go watch it right now! Then, when you worry, think of that instead. Heck, go watch

it again if you can. Or pick something non-panda that tickles your brain, something you want to think about that will kick the troll right the heck out of your mind.

SELF-ADORNMENT *IS* SELF-CARE

Getting dressed up, putting on your favorite jewels, coifing your amazing rainbow locks. It feels *good*. Self-adornment has been going on since ancient times, with charcoal eyeliner, feather hair accessories, and bone and stone jewelry. It's sometimes thought of as fashion and style—usually by haters with no sense of style— but it has endured because it's really a form of self-care. The perfect dress can empower you, a bold gold necklace can be your good luck charm, a great mani-hoofi can have therapeutic effects. Self-adornment brings out the magical unicorn in us all! Here are some unicorntastic self-adornments to check out:

- ♥ crystal jewelry (see page 143 for crystal power)
- ♥ rainbow hair chalk or dye
- ♥ shimmery eyeshadow
- ♥ feather hairclips
- ♥ aromatherapy-diffuser necklaces
- ♥ magnetic manicures (the metallic shimmer gets patterned by magnets!)
- ♥ alicorn headbands
- ♥ flower crowns
- ♥ rainbow leggings
- ♥ sequined slip-ons

A unicorn's horn is called an alicorn.

- ♡ mood rings
- ♡ faux-fur jackets
- ♡ dragon or unicorn ear clips that climb from your lobes to your head
- ♡ intricate braids woven with ribbon
- ♡ copper-colored mirror-lens sunglasses
- ♡ glitter on everything!

UNICORN HAIR

Is there anything lovelier or more enchanting than rainbow locks, a rose-gold mane, or some braids shot through with purple? If you want to charm your hair into a cascade of colors, it's probably easier than you think. To get the look just for the day, check out hair chalks; they give just a dust of hue on any color of hair, and they're as easy to use as crayons. You can also find hairsprays in myriad colors, pastel and neon, as well as with glitter. The only downside is that they leave your hair looking a little glued together.

If your current hair color is on the lighter side, there are some amazing colored conditioning rinses that come in the entire rainbow of hues. These nourish your hair while giving it a magical look. (If your hair is dark, these will show up as a tint in the sunshine—and there are a lot of nice things to say about that subtlety!) If you're a brunette but want the really bright or really pastel colors, that's when things get a little trickier, as you'll have to bring in some bleach. And when chemicals are called for, you should consider also calling in a professional.

THE IMPORTANCE OF BEING ARTY

Having a creative outlet is good for the spirit. Getting into the flow of making something puts you on that magical wavelength of oneness with the world, and the stress just pours out of you. It's a therapy, a hobby, and a happy place all rolled into one. But don't think for a second that "art" needs to be painting or sculpting or anything else traditionally thought of as Art with a capital A. Your art form can be anything that is creative and that you enjoy.

Cooking is an excellent example of art. You get your hands dirty, you work with interesting tools and media, it's super shareable, and its impermanence is freeing. It doesn't have to be absolutely neat or perfect to be amazing.

Journaling is an art, as is **scrapbooking** and any other way in which you transmute your thoughts to paper. If you're really into these arts, buying books with really nice paper stock and investing in a fancy pen make the whole act feel more enchanting.

Dancing is an amazing art. It gets your blood going and gets you out of your head and into your body. There are so many styles, and once you get some basic moves down, the whole world of dance opens.

Painting and **sculpting** are considered Art with a capital A by most, but that shouldn't make you shy away from them. They are millennia-old art forms, and you can take them as seriously or as playfully as you want. There is infinite inspiration out there for what you can represent through these arts, and there's no right or wrong way to do them.

Collaging used to be huge, and not just with teenagers. In modern art, it can absolutely get a capital A, because you can take so much wide-ranging cultural imagery and fit it together. It can be fun and humorous or momentous and memorial. It is an art of patience and precision.

Felting is a super-cool way to turn wool into 3-D figures that are often absolutely adorable. Little fuzzy lambs and dogs, gnomes with pointy hats, and unicorns with pointy horns. Really, if you can imagine it, you can felt it.

Dioramas are not just for school projects. Creating little worlds with moods and magic all their own is incredibly satisfying, and you can put literally anything you want into them.

Making **miniatures** from polymer clay is a really huge trend right now (punicorn most certainly intended). There are a ton of great tutorials for making everything from teeny-tiny foods to super-small creatures to magically mini manga characters.

Cross-stitching is having a renaissance of cool. From enchanting forest scenes to sassy messaging (you've gotta Google this!) to Americana throwback designs, making your own fabric art is well loved these days and well worth a try.

Mosaics make for awesome home décor. Outdoor spaces, flower pots, and kitchen and bathroom surfaces can all be personalized with a little tile, a little grout, and the spark of an idea.

UNICORN YOUR VACATION

There are a few key ways to unicorn your vacation, to make it the most magical that it can possibly be, but it all starts with knowing what "vacation" means to you(nicorn). You have to decide if you want to go relax somewhere beautiful where your every need is attended to and you don't have to worry about a single thing, or if you want to go to a city with hustle and bustle and culture and shows and music and museums, or if you want to get out into the wild and feel the earth beneath your hoofs.

Once you know what kind of vacation you want, consider dabbling in the nearly extinct mystical practice of hiring a travel agent. You may think you can't afford one, but the truth is a pro can save you so much money on your actual trip that they pay for themselves while charting out the best experience possible. No longer do you have to rely on persnickety online reviews left by irritable imps and unreliable minotaurs who are irrationally angry about an unimpressive hedge maze. Get a grip, bullies! Instead, someone with real knowledge of a place will help you tailor-make a perfect trip.

Plan a splurge. Find a place you really want to see, a thing you really want to do, a restaurant you really want to eat at that is beyond your regular price range and just do it. While you're there, really take your time and soak it in. Make it memorable.

It could be one of those things you always look back on and think, "Dang, I'm so glad I did that!"

Make some friends while you're on your trip. You're in a new place, and there are lots of creatures there whom you'll only have this one chance to talk to. Find out about them and where they come from. See whether they have discovered any magic in the place that you haven't seen yet.

Most importantly, leave your regular life at home. Don't check your e-mail frantically or text lots of people or post and post and post to social media. Those things all smack of your everyday life, and a vacation is supposed to be a break from just that. Limit or totally nix screen time. If worries about work or anything else creep in, actively push them out. Picture yourself kicking them right out a window. Let yourself really soak up the new place— how it looks, how it feels, how it smells, how it sparkles.

FROLICKING:
A HOW-TO GUIDE

We all need to frolic more. It's soooo good for keeping your horn held high and your magic reserves topped off, and odds are you haven't frolicked in ages, maybe even since you were a kid. Well, today is a new day: the day you start frolicking! Now is the time to remember what it's like to be outside and just frickin' loving it, running around soaking up the sun and the breeze and the air, watching the flowers and the critters running hither and thither. Magic!

FROLIC LIKE NOBODY IS WATCHING

Just be there and let loose! Ignore anyone else who may be around, because if they don't get frolicking, then nuts to them! (See page 71 for more on that.)

To frolic effectively, you're going to need a pretty place to do it. An enchanted forest is ideal, though a park can work quite nicely. To really get into it, consider dressing for the occasion in gauzy, flowy materials that will trail after you and blow around in the breeze. I won't say you *have* to wear a flower crown, but you absolutely should wear a flower crown (see page 70). Making it on location from flowers that are permissible for picking is a bonus.

OK, you're at the place of merriment. You're dressed for frolicking. Now, all you need to do is kick off your shoes—being barefoot really helps—and just start skipping and cavorting, jumping and running. Bring a friend or a dog or some other creature and chase them. Have them chase you.

A FLOWERING CROWN FOR YOUR HAPPY HEAD

Flowers are beautiful, they smell great, and you can wear them on your head. What more can you ask for from nature? Flower crowns are a magical way to wreath yourself in beauty and enjoy the wonder that are blossoms. There are a few ways to make them, but step one is always to get a bunch of flowers.

If you have flowers with long stems, such as daisies, you can go old-fashioned and au naturel. One way to make a crown is to take the three flowers with the longest stems and braid the stems together for about one inch. Then lay another flower on the braid and begin braiding that flower stem in with the others. Keep going until you have the length you like and tuck the remaining stems into the top flowers where you started. Voilà!

Another all-natural way to make a crown from long-stemmed flowers is by using either your fingernail or a knife to make a small slit in a flower's stem just below the bloom. Slip a second flower through the slit and then make a slit in that flower's stem. Keep on slitting and slipping until the chain is as long as you want it to be, and then make a second slit in the stem of the first flower to slip the stem of the final flower through it.

If you want to use lots of different flowers, regardless of the state of their stems, you can make a base for your crown using floral wire, then attach the flowers to the wire by wrapping floral tape around whatever stems they have and your wire base.

THE MAGICAL ART OF GIVING ZERO FUDGES

There are opinions that matter—your own, those of the people whom you love and who love you, respectable colleagues, trusted friends—and opinions that don't. The magical art of giving zero fudges is all about having absolutely no care for and giving no thought to the opinions of strangers, haters, naysayers, and other decidedly treacherous or irrelevant creatures. Because the thing about the opinions of folks in those categories is that you're probably imagining them for the most part anyway. Strangers don't often tell you what they're thinking; you might just guess or assume they're thinking something negative about you because you're letting your unicorn flag fly or you're frolicking with abandon and they are looking your way. They might have a look on their face that seems a bit judgy. Or they might be taking some sidelong glances. Or they might just be blank. You can easily project any fear you have about what folks might think of you onto their faces. It's too easy to do. But in fact, you're just making up stories. You have no idea what's going on in their domes. So why bother? Why give something like that any power, or any fudges for that matter?

There will, of course, be the times in your unicorn life when you do encounter a negative gnome or a downer demon who

tells you exactly what they're thinking and it isn't exactly a compliment. It is so, so hard to let an insult or slight slide. You might mull over those nasty words again and again and again. This is when you really need the magical art of giving zero fudges. And like all magical arts, it's easier said than done.

First you need to remember that not everyone's opinions should matter to you. If they don't know you or they themselves are more cruel than kind, then you shouldn't give them any of your power or energy. And when you let someone get under your hide, that's exactly what you're doing: giving them the power to affect your thoughts and take up your precious mental energy.

If you find yourself falling into a troll hole of reflecting on someone's ill treatment of you, then you have to climb and scrape your way out. Pick a thought that delights you (see the pandas on page 59), a memory that you love, or a compliment you received that means a lot to you and focus on that. Your mind will try to drag you back down into the troll hole over and over again, but it's *your* mind. You own that thing, and you steer it. So steer it somewhere wonderful that's well away from the words of creeps. They don't deserve any of your fudges!

UNICORN YOUR RELATIONSHIPS

YOUR FRIENDS, FAMILY, AND LOVED ones are likely an amazing and varied herd of magical beasts. They might not all be unicorns, but they all have their own powers. You probably wish you could be squeezing some of them right now in an enormous hug. Some of them, maybe not so much. Some of them are amazing from the moment you meet them and you lock into a simpatico mental wavelength, feeling like you can beam messages directly from horn to horn—you're always on the same page of your fairy tale. With others you just don't know what the heck is going on in that lovely head of theirs.

This chapter will give you some inspiration to show your appreciation for the spellbinding awesomeness and charms of your unicorn friends. You are magical cohorts and so should do some magical things together! Same goes for that special someone. There are so many ways to add enchantments to romances, whether they be new or long term—even if the sparkle seems like it's dulled a bit, you'll find plenty of ways to reignite the magic.

If it's new blood you're looking for, whether that means friendship or something more, there are special unicorn ways of finding like-minded creatures, sparking new friendships, and homing in on future honey bunnies. Why not expand your realm of familiars?

Family ties can be the strongest magic in the land, as well as the most infuriating. Boosting the best and withstanding the worst is what unicorns do with their blood ties. Whether you can't get enough of that rascally bunch or, well, the opposite of that, you'll learn how to make the most of your relationships with your kin.

The thing about other creatures—family, friends, beloveds, or mortal enemies—is that you can't control them. The trick and truth of a good relationship is to not let that scuff your horn. They are who they are. Trolls are trolls, fairies are fairies, ogres are ogres, and if you figure out who someone is and accept it, instead of expecting or hoping they will act differently, or take your advice, or change one day, you'll be a lot happier and your relationship will be a lot more awesome. This chapter will give you some ways of figuring out how to handle the more tumultuous relationships so you can be awesomely you and keep on with your enchanted fairy tale of life, no matter what those around you try to do.

BUF (BEST UNICORN FRIEND) LEGENDS AND MYTHS

Having a BUF, the unicorn equivalent of a BFF, can be awesome. Someone you can tell anything to, feel totally comfortable around, count on to help you out in a jam or make you laugh when you're down—someone like that makes life more shimmery and magical. But how do you know when someone is your BUF? Maybe it's really obvious; maybe you've known your BUF since

you were just colts and don't have to think twice about the question. But maybe you're not so sure of the answer because there are a few creatures who could qualify, or your level of closeness to various unicorns shifts over time.

The truth is that while the idea of a BUF is super fun, you don't have to put that label on any one friendship. By definition, you can have only one BUF, because "best" means *the* most awesome and excellent and limits you to just one friend for the job. But you can have lots of friends who feel like the best! You can be close to someone on and off for lots of reasons. Or you might be part of a group of friends and one could or would want to pick out a favorite. In those cases, putting the BUF label on a friendship can be complicated, erroneous, or even hurtful to some unicorns you love. So if the horseshoe fits, wear it. But if it's making your hoof hurt, just forget it and embrace all your friends without trying to jam them into some idea they don't fit into.

FRIEND APPRECIATION

Showing appreciation and love to your friends is straight-up fun! You think they rock, and by doing something special to show them that, you'll feel great and they'll feel great. Plus, thinking about how cool a friend is and all the things you could do to delight them is a really entertaining and rewarding way to spend your time. If you're feeling down, it makes a surprisingly good pick-me-up to plan a pick-me-up for someone else! It's a win-win.

Showing a friend a little love can take a ton of forms. Just picture your friend and all the things that make them happy, then make a plan that revolves all around them. These can be big days or just little bits of hidden magic to make your fellow unicorn smile. Here are a few ideas to get you started:

- ♥ plan a movie night with your friend's favorite flicks and snacks
- ♥ hide their favorite kind of candy bar somewhere in their home
- ♥ make their favorite meal or take them out to their favorite restaurant
- ♥ if you've been friends forever, take them to a cherished spot from your shared childhood
- ♥ send them flowers or candy or some little token you know they'll love
- ♥ plan a spa day

- ♡ sign both of you up for one of those art classes that is essentially an excuse to drink wine
- ♡ put together a friendship photo album with real, actual, physical photos
- ♡ have a craft day
- ♡ go hiking
- ♡ put together matching outfits
- ♡ go karaoke-ing
- ♡ put together a playlist you know they'll love
- ♡ dance party!!!
- ♡ get all glittered up for a night on the town
- ♡ write to their favorite celebrity asking for an autograph (you'd be surprised by how many will oblige)
- ♡ bake them some cookies
- ♡ make them a friendship bracelet
- ♡ send them a singing telegram (yes, they still exist, and you may even get the messenger to wear a unicorn costume)
- ♡ plant some flowers in their yard when they aren't home (tip: yellow roses symbolize friendship)
- ♡ send a card for no other reason than to tell them they're awesome
- ♡ enter a three-legged race or some other kind of competition that calls for a duo
- ♡ plan a surprise party for their next birthday
- ♡ hide sticky notes with funny and/or thankful messages in their car, their bag, or wherever they'll be surprised to find them
- ♡ make a donation in their name to a cause they care about

- 💟 show up with a bottle of wine
- 💟 think of something they've always wanted to do—learn to knit, go skydiving, bake a soufflé—and make it happen
- 💟 make polymer-clay charms together (if you don't know what that is, do an image search right now—they are so easy and so squee!)
- 💟 offer to help them clean their closet (this is something everyone needs)
- 💟 send a text message that says "You're so cool!" or something similar that will make them smile

IS IT IN THE STARS?

There are so many reasons to get along—or not—with your fellow creatures. Some say that whether relationships sparkle—or dull—is written in the stars. If you want to turn to the universe for some clues on compatibility, you may want to take a look at your zodiac sign and see how it matches up—or doesn't—with someone else's.

The signs all fall into different elemental categories, and those who share an element have good magical odds of getting along. The elements are as follows.

Fire includes the signs Aries, Leo, and Sagittarius, which are a smart, spirited, creative, and active lot. They may anger easily, but they cool down just as fast.

Earth signs are Taurus, Virgo, and Capricorn. They are a down-to-earth group; loyal and practical, they are great problem solvers to have on your side, even if they can be a bit emotional.

Air elementals are Gemini, Libra, and Aquarius, social creatures who love a spirited debate and a killer party. They are great at giving advice but sometimes like the sounds of their own voices a bit too much.

Water signs are Cancer, Scorpio, and Pisces, and they know exactly what you're thinking. They are that intuitive. They are so good to those they love, and they revel in intimacy, but they can also be super sensitive.

If you share the exact same sign with someone else, you may have some issues that come from being too alike. Your faults are their faults, so you may not counterbalance each other when it comes to shortcomings. On the plus side, you likely have a ton in common, and when it comes to your positive points, your powers combined earn compound interest.

No signs can be said to be completely incompatible. It's more like there's a range of likely compatibility. Even if you're polar opposites, your differences may dovetail nicely to form a perfect whole like yin and yang. Check out the star chart to see how likely you are to get along with other signs.

MAGICAL STAR CONNECTIONS

Them \ You(nicorn)	Aries ♈	Taurus ♉	Gemini ♊	Cancer ♋	Leo ♌	Virgo ♍	Libra ♎	Scorpio ♏	Sagittarius ♐	Capricorn ♑	Aquarius ♒	Pisces ♓
Aries ♈	★	★	★	★	≫★	★	★	★	≫★	★	★	★
Taurus ♉	★	≫★	★	★	★	≫★	★	★	★	≫★	★	★
Gemini ♊	★	★	≫★	★	★	★	≫★	★	★	★	≫★	★
Cancer ♋	★	★	★	≫★	★	★	★	≫★	★	★	★	≫★
Leo ♌	≫★	★	★	★	≫★	★	★	★	≫★	★	★	★
Virgo ♍	★	≫★	★	★	★	≫★	★	★	★	≫★	★	★
Libra ♎	★	★	≫★	★	★	★	≫★	★	★	≫★	★	★
Scorpio ♏	★	★	★	≫★	★	★	★	≫★	★	★	★	≫★
Sagittarius ♐	≫★	★	★	★	≫★	★	★	★	≫★	★	★	★
Capricorn ♑	★	≫★	★	★	★	≫★	★	★	★	≫★	★	★
Aquarius ♒	★	★	≫★	★	★	★	≫★	★	★	★	≫★	★
Pisces ♓	★	★	★	≫★	★	★	★	≫★	★	★	★	≫★

STAR POWER KEY

★ not great	★ good stuff
★ meh	≫★ AMAZING!
★ pretty OK	

FARAWAY FRIENDS

Sometimes friends move away. It sucks, but it happens. And when it does, it can take a little piece of your heart somewhere far away. Staying in touch today is easier than it's ever been with all the digital means of communication that are at our hooftips pretty much 24/7, but sometimes these things can also make it easy to forget to have meaningful communication. Liking a

photo or commenting on a post isn't nearly as good as actually having a conversation with someone. So even if you feel like you're keeping up on a faraway friend's activities, make sure you keep up on making meaningful connections with them as well.

This can mean getting on the phone or, even better, having a video call. If you can make it a regular event, it will keep you close even over the distance of an ocean or a continent. And that's pretty much magic! Sending care packages, as the name indicates, is another way to show you care. It doesn't have to be big or expensive or even hand-packed. You can buy a nearly infinite number of sparkly, adorable things on the Internet and have them shipped around the world for cheap or free. Even just a postcard shows you're thinking extra about someone.

Just because you can't hang out face to face doesn't mean you can't do things together. Plan to watch the same movie at the same time. Read the same book and have a book club. Have taco Tuesdays and experiment with the same recipes in your separate kitchens. Share a playlist. Listen to the same podcasts. Wear matching or conjoining friendship bracelets or charms. You can still share activities you love even if you aren't together.

And whenever it's possible, get together! If you can swing it, show up for a holiday or event but don't tell them you're coming. "Far away" doesn't have to be all the time and forever.

FRIENDSHIP CALENDAR

If you find you're so busy that you don't see your friends as much as you'd like, or if you're missing certain friends who are hard to see because of busy schedules, then you need a friendship calendar! Start by listing all the people you'd like to hang out with. Go through the contact list on your phone and your friend lists on social media to find hidden gems you might not think of often enough. Identify the approximate date you last saw each chum. If you can't even remember when you last saw someone, then be extra glad they're on your list, because that means you're going to see them soon!

Next, get a calendar of your choice. This may be a physical wall calendar or an online one; use whatever works best for you and keep it in a way that means you'll actually look at it and use it. Now, start writing people's names on days when you're going to reach out to them. You can start reaching out as soon as you like—today, even! When the day does come to say hello, you can call, text, e-mail, do whatever you like, but make it a goal of your communication to set up some sort of hangout and put that on your friend calendar. If they're too far away to set up a horn-to-horn meeting, then figure out something you can do together while apart (see page 86). If you don't get in touch with them on the day you plan or if a hangout falls through, your calendar will help you keep on top of rescheduling your playdate.

REKINDLING OLD MAGIC

It's easy to lose touch with old friends. Life gets busy, people move, little ones are born, jobs get demanding, moves happen—there are a ton of reasons that can lead to you waking up in the morning and realizing you haven't seen someone you absolutely adore in years. But you don't have to let friends slip away! It will take some work and planning and routine breaking and maybe even traveling, but if you really cherished someone once, it's worth trying to get that old spark back in your heart.

When you do arrange to meet an old friend (or even just get on the phone if a horn-to-horn meeting is impossible), that

old magic may be right there on the surface, glittering back to glorious life in no time. Or it might take a little time to find it again. Catching up on current events is necessary and great, but if you're having trouble getting into your old groove, play the "Remember when . . ." game. A trip down memory lane is an easy way to reconnect and remember why you got along so famously to begin with.

Be prepared, though, that sometimes you can't relive the magic of yesterday. You're both different creatures than you once were, and you might not connect as hard and fast as you once did. Even if this is the case, you don't need to be disappointed. Just because things aren't what they used to be doesn't mean that what they are now isn't valuable or worth experiencing. You may find a whole new friend in an old friend if you are prepared to accept them for who they are now and don't hold on too tightly to who they were in the old days.

NEXT STOP: MEMORY LANE

Break out some old photos if you have them, or check out an old haunt together. Conjure up those little magic moments you had together.

SHUT UP AND LISTEN

Sorry to speak so harshly, but this is a hard—and important—lesson to learn! When someone you love tells you about a problem they have, your instinct is probably to try to help them fix it. You're probably brimming with useful advice on what they could do to get out of their jam or make their bad situation better. The solution might be oh so obvious to you! But please, please, please, just shut up. Whether or not you have the perfect advice is, at least for this moment, absolutely irrelevant. Your loved one, in all likelihood, just needs to vent, and that venting is important. Saying something out loud, getting it out of your head and into the open, is a necessary step in working through a problem. It's therapeutic, even. If you keep jumping in with your two gold pieces, you could very well frustrate instead of help. Your loved one needs a sounding board more than they need advice. If a solution is obvious to you, it likely is or will become obvious to them in the course of talking about it.

So if you get a call that starts, "You will never believe what happened to me!" the first thing you need to do is open your ears and shut your mouth. Let your loved one run their full course of complaint. Ask questions, but don't give answers unless they're asked for. Once the venting runs out of steam, ask your friend whether they have a plan. If they do, listen to it the whole way through, and if it's a good plan, say so. If it's not, gently offer refinement that you think will help. There's no need to criticize their plan as you do this. And if you're at all in doubt, you can always ask them whether they want advice or just need to let it all out.

IDENTIFYING OTHER UNICORNS IN THE WILD

Making a new friend or finding a new love interest is sometimes as easy as saying hi to another unicorn and feeling that magic spark of kindred spirit—you just frickin' know you were meant to be friends or something more. But it's not always super easy to spot those magical fellow beasts, nor is the spark always instantaneous and obvious. Relationships are gold, though, and it's worth a little bit of effort to be on the lookout for new ones.

Friends and more-than-friends come in all shapes and sizes, which is rad, but it can make them hard to spot. At a class, at work, or at a local watering hole—anywhere you see the same people on the reg—is the easiest place to zero in on a future friend. Forget about appearance, status, and all that noise. Instead, look at body language and reactions. Do you and someone else think the same things are funny? Do you roll your eyes at the same stuff? Do your ears prick up to the same songs? There are all sorts of things you can have in common that lie below the surface.

Making first real contact can be a little challenging. Casual hellos are one thing, but to break the ice with your majestic golden horn and get down deeper to find out whether you have the stuff of a relationship in common can take time. Lots of folks are their public selves at first, and it takes some time to find the real unicorn who lives below the protective shell. The fastest way to crack through is to be your most natural self. That means breaking open your own candy coating and being open to revealing the true marzipan within.

Some good ways to break through to the true are by offering a kindness. Share some gum or a snack. Offer to get someone a coffee or tea if you're getting one for yourself. Ask what song someone would love to hear and then go play it on the jukebox. A compliment is also a great convo starter, as long as it's genuine. If you've noticed something you both have in common, chat about that. Try to find something positive if you take this tack. It's easy to complain about stuff, even with strangers, but it's a lot more meaningful and better for your spirit if you can bond over something you love rather than something you hate. If you think you may like, *like like* the creature in question, you might be extra nervous to make these moves, but confidence is the sexiest thing a unicorn can have. Also, embrace the cliché "fake it 'til you make it."

Once a crack in the icy public shell starts to form, exchange info and set up a super-casual playdate. Don't do something that's going to last too long, and try to choose a place that will be equally comfortable for you both. Maybe there's

a café you both like or have been meaning to try. If you sense someone is shy, maybe don't go to your favorite hang spot where you're sure to see a bunch of people you know. Meeting a hundred new faces might overwhelm some folk. On the other hand, if they're a socialicorn, your friend hotspot might be just the ticket. (This tactic could work for potential love interests as well as future friends.)

MAGICAL DATES

Whether your beloved is new to you(nicorn) or a long-term honey, there's nothing like a truly magical date. They are some of life's best and sparkliest gems, even if they aren't with the creature who turns out to be your forevericorn. Sometimes they are first dates, sometimes they are celebratory of anniversaries or good tidings, and sometimes they just come out of the blue. While a magical date can happen spontaneously through nothing more than a confluence of good moods and luck, you can also plan to make a date something special. Here are a few ideas to put you on Romance Road:

THE TRUE CHARM

What makes a date really magical is the connection you make with the creature you're with. And you're more likely to feel that spark if you're *doing* something together. Dinner and a movie are nice, but adventure is the true charm. So get off your tails and find some exploits!

- 💜 check out a winery
- 💜 take a dance class, such as salsa or tango
- 💜 go to a sculpture garden
- 💜 play laser tag
- 💜 take a cooking class
- 💜 couple's massage!!!
- 💜 find a fireworks display
- 💜 sit by a fire
- 💜 dress each other up for a night on the town
- 💜 head to the beach at night and bring sparklers
- 💜 go skydiving!
- 💜 have a picnic next to a river
- 💜 go on a stargazing tour
- 💜 take a sunset cruise
- 💜 watch the dawn from the quietest place you can think of

KEYS TO THE COMMUNICATION KINGDOM

You always hear that communication is the key to a healthy and lasting relationship, and they couldn't be more correct. If you're not communicating effectively, you could very well dull all the good, glittery bits of your relationship. Keeping your thoughts and feelings trapped in your own head leads to all sorts of problems. If they're good thoughts, they deserve to be let out where they can soar and be majestic. You might be afraid of expressing emotions your partner perhaps doesn't share; while it's true that you might not be evenly matched in how much you care for each other, it's better to know that than to pretend otherwise. If you're having problems, they will only grow and fester if left in the dark, becoming more beastly than need be. Give your partner the chance to respond to your concerns. You may be surprised at the results, and even if you're not, you'll feel so much lighter after you unburden yourself.

The unicorn's honest truth is that a relationship's maximum possible level of happiness is limited when one or more people in that relationship keep secrets. Keeping your lips sealed about being angry over one issue could mean you explode with fantastic rage over something unrelated. Not expressing the fullness of your heart could make you sad or cause you to act in ways that are not true to your heart and horn. This can in turn cause your partner to wonder all sorts of things about what's going on in your head. Love can only really live in the light, and secrets and hidden feelings bring only darkness.

It's all well and good to know that you should be communicating your hopes, fears, feelings, and problems with your partner, but this is another mega case of "easier said than done." (Or, actually, not easily said in this case.) It might be that you get nervous and don't say what you truly mean, or you don't reveal the full truth. There are a few things you can do to help get the words out, even when you are super nervous.

First, be brutally honest with yourself. Sometimes when you want a relationship to work badly enough, you may lie even in your own head, heart, and horn about how you feel. Or you may let bad behavior slide, making excuses for it. For a relationship to really work, you need to be honest with yourself and your partner. They will respect you for it, and respect is another big key to happy hearts.

Plan a time to talk. Things will go more smoothly if you know you'll have the time and privacy to have the discussion you need. Blurting out something in a restaurant because you just couldn't keep it in anymore will only make things harder on both of you.

Write down what you want to say. This will not only help you have the discussion but will also super help you process your own feelings. You may discover things you didn't even realize when the words were only in your mind. You can bring a bulleted list of what you want to say to the talk itself if you like—a fully prepared speech, on the other hand, might get derailed in a horn-to-horn discussion. You can also send your partner an e-mail or letter with the main points you want to discuss if you're afraid you won't be able to say them all when the time comes to talk. But if you do this, you still need to talk, out loud, with your mouths.

When you do sit down to talk, staying calm may not be possible through the whole discussion, but it's something to strive for. If you make it a point to be as cool horned as you can, you'll be less likely to say something you don't mean. Letting something slip out in anger or frustration means you just end up with more to discuss, as apologies are made and true intent is explained. Try to listen as much as you talk. Let your partner finish what they're saying, really consider what they've said, and try your best to see things from their perspective. Defensiveness and believing you know what they're thinking or saying no matter the words that are coming out of their mouth will just lead to more issues.

All these practices should be a two-way street. Be honest with your partner and trust them to be honest in return. If they aren't treating you with the honesty or respect you're giving them, that alone should make you think long and hard about whether your partner is right for you.

Getting on the path of communication can be hard if you're in a relationship that's been close lipped for a long time. If this is the case, couple's counseling can be really valuable. Someone with experience facilitating hard discussions can help you both open up your hearts.

ARE YOU MY SOULMATE?

So you think you may have found the *one*! That sparkly, magical, iridescent romanticorn you want to spend the rest of your life with. *But how do you really know?* you may wonder. There are so many love stories about couples just knowing from the first glance or at some amazing moment that they would be together forever. While that may be true on the rarest of occasions, odds are even if that's the story a couple is sticking with, they've probably had a flicker or two of private doubt—doubt that they don't mention because it might tarnish their shiny love story.

While every relationship is different, with different strengths and weaknesses and ways of expressing love and being together, there are a few good indications that you've found your soulmateicorn. First, you're friends. Granted, you are more than friends, but part of your desire to be with them is that they have all the characteristics of being your best friend. You love hanging out with them, you can tell them anything, and when you're with them it feels natural and homey.

Second, you respect each other. You think they're the coolest, and they think the same about you. You love the kind of decisions they make and the things they do. Not every single one and all the time, but you definitely trust them to do the right thing most of the time.

You also get each other. You each understand what makes the other tick, what tickles your respective funny bones, and what really ticks the other off. This doesn't mean you can read each other's minds or are always certain of how the other will react, but you get the big picture of who you are, who they are, and who you are together as a couple.

Wanting the same things in a big-picture way is also important. If you love, love, *love* your partner, but they want kids and you don't, or you want to live in the city but they are really only happy in the forest, or you live to travel and they have anxiety about it, or all you ever want to do is be out and about amongst creatures and they just want to stay home snuggling on the couch . . . well, these are important considerations. Love is the most important thing, but being in a relationship that allows you each to live the life you need to live to be true to yourselves is right up there at the top of the list too.

Finally, do you really feel like you around your potential soulmate? If the answer is emphatically yes, then wahoo! That's great! If you feel like you have to put on an act or tamp down parts of your magical, majestic personality around them, that is potentially a problem. You owe it to each other and yourselves to each be your true self when you're together. That's the only way you'll be able to know if it's true love.

A UNICORN IS A UNICORN, A TROLL IS A TROLL

Some creatures' behavior can be confusing, infuriating, exasperating, or even enraging. Here's the hard truth, though: you and you alone are in charge of how you feel. The world is a wild and magical and unfair and beautiful and complicated place. The only thing you can control is your reaction to it.

When fellow creatures act in ways you wouldn't or don't approve of, it's easy to get all riled up. Instead of letting your knee be jerked in reaction to someone's behavior, try to take a step back and understand why they are behaving that way. If they are a mean-spirited troll who takes pleasure in being awful or intimidating or overpowering, then that's who they are. And you are who you are: a beautiful and strong unicorn who does not need to lower yourself to the shortcomings of others. Why be provoked by a troll? More to the point, why expect a troll to behave in any other way than like a troll?

If you meet creatures where they are and understand them for what they are, you'll have a much easier time of dealing with them. That doesn't mean they won't get under your hide every now and again, but if you just take a deep breath and remember their nature, then you won't take their behavior so personally or be as affected by it.

KEEPING THE MAGIC ALIVE

Being with the same romanticorn for a long time is, in itself, pretty magical. Having someone whom you can depend on, who knows you down to your core as you know them, and with whom your love is as fundamental a reality as the color of the sky and the movement of the tides is straight-up amazing. But the flip side of that golden coin is that when something becomes a bedrock in your life, you can forget to notice how shiny it is. Things can become everyday

instead of hooray, and that jittery, anticipatory excitement of a fresh relationship calms.

That's not inherently bad, but it's more fun—as well as good for the heart and horn—if you make sure to acknowledge the grandeur that is your love at least every now and again. You can do so with big gestures or by recognizing the small things you share that feel like magic, like your morning rituals or your ability to secretly communicate through subtle body language. Here are some activities two unicorns can do to keep the magic alive:

go on an annivesarymoon

take a bath together, complete with glitter bath bomb

plan a surprise anything

do something that's a favorite of your partner's but that you don't often do because you find it to be meh—and really make an effort to enjoy it with them

keep fit together

do something completely new to both of you

write a love letter or a list of all the things that make your partner the frickin' coolest

make a soundtrack of your relationship that's got all the songs that have been important to you

make your partner heart-shaped foods, which are silly and small but super effective

FAMILY BLESSINGS

☆ ☆ ☆
☆ ☆

A group of unicorns is called a blessing, so your family is, believe it or not, a blessing! You might not be convinced that they're all unicorns, and maybe some of them better fit into other creature categories, but you're all of the same stock, and you're probably stuck with them for life, so you best make the most of it.

If you basically get along with your blessing, then showing them appreciation will come easily. Brighten someone's day by making a little bit of magic for them with some flowers or a sweet note thanking them for just being them. Whether you're keeping in touch, lending a hand, sharing meals, celebrating holidays, or whatever else it is you like to do with your blessing, try to always give at least one quick thought of appreciation for your loved ones.

Long-distant familial relations can be tough, with lots of missing others and feelings of homesickness. Regular video chatting is a good way to keep in touch, so try to do it regularly and even spontaneously. If you're somewhere really beautiful that your momicorn would love, video call her from your phone, just for a minute or two. Technology can be magical, and when used this way it can close great distances.

WHEN FAMILY IS A PAIN IN THE HORN

Some families, or members of families, can really get your goat. There is a wide spectrum of really irritating to real dysfunction. If your family falls into true dysfunction, therapy can be a big relief. Whether you go as a group or pursue it on your own, it is vital in dealing and living with hardships.

If, on the other hoof, your family or members thereof are more on the purely exasperating end of the spectrum, there are a few things you can try to do to temper your frustrations. First, don't expect them to be anyone but who they are. If you know they do certain things that drive you up the wall, just accept them as givens and move the heck on. (For more on this, see page 107.) Try to focus, instead, on something positive about them. Find something, anything that you have in common or that is cool about them—there has to be *something*—and try to make conversations and interactions involve that thing.

If they love to talk (or argue with you) about something that makes you totally crazed, such as politics, money, or what you *should* be doing, tell them, gently, that you understand their point of view but that going over the same old ground won't get either of you anywhere, so why not talk about something else? If they refuse to be derailed, let them know that you'll have to excuse yourself if the conversation doesn't change. If they don't stop, make good on your promise.

Unicorn Fact!

Marco Polo
thought he saw
unicorns on his
travels, but what
he had really
seen was their
surly cousin, the
rhinoceros.

IDENTIFYING ENERGY VAMPIRES

Part of accepting creatures for what they truly are is understanding what they are. There are all sorts of types in the world, including the infamous energy vampire. These creatures glom on to others and try to suck out their energy. They are creatures of almost pure need, and they wield guilt and manipulation like blood-sucking fangs. You can identify the energy vampire by their excessive tellings of woe-is-me stories: if you meet someone who is eager to tell you about all their troubles and how unfairly life has treated them, you may have an energy vampire on your hands. They will usually, in just a short time, begin asking for favors, which often get bigger and bigger and more imposing in just a short while. You might find yourself compelled to oblige them because you feel guilty or sorry for them.

It's possible to have a real relationship with an energy vampire, but remember that relationships are two-way streets in which, ideally, you are giving as much as you're getting. Or if that's not the case, you should at least feel comfortable in the relationship. If your relationship with someone is based mostly on you sympathizing with them as they complain about every little thing, that's not good. If you often feel ill at ease and put upon by them, if you suspect they are manipulating you into doing things for them, if they get mad at you when you can't do

something for them even if you have a good reason, then that's not a relationship. If they do something for you, especially something you didn't ask for, and then use the supposed kindness to get you to do something for them, that's not OK.

When confronted with an energy vampire, you are well within your rights to cut off their supply of energy or guilt-induced favors. You don't have to be in a relationship with someone who habitually makes you feel bad or takes without giving in a way that drains you of your own life force. If you want to try to maintain a relationship because they have positive points and you feel a genuine love for them—and not just a genuine pity— then the next time they begin to complain about something, cut them off when they start. Acknowledge that they feel bad and then suggest that talking about something else will get their mind off their troubles. Keep moving the conversation on. You can be honest with them that, for your own sake, you need to focus on the positive at the moment and doing so will be good for you both.

If they want a favor you aren't happy to do for them, then tell them that you're unable to help them this time. If someone truly cares for you as you do for them, they will understand and not want to put you out. You have to be as open about your needs and feelings as the energy vampire is about their own.

BATTLING EVIL

Unicorns are pure and magical creatures of the light who sparkle with their lovely coolness. But that doesn't mean they are without enemies. There are dark creatures in the world, and though they may be misunderstood and in some ways worthy of sympathy and kindness, you need to draw a line—you can't give up too much of your magic for the sake of others.

We've talked about the energy vampire and how to handle them, but what about mean creatures who seem like they're out to get you? The ones who decide to be your enemy and won't let you play any other role? Accepting them for who they are and feeling sorry for them for having to be miserable instead of

awesome will only get you so far, and it won't necessarily protect you from bullying attacks.

If you find yourself on the receiving end of someone's anger, whether IRL or online, it can really shake you. Even if you understand on a rational level that an attack boils down to their own issues, they've made their problem your problem, and you need to protect yourself. If it's a one-off situation, like an angry ogre in a store or on the road, the best thing you can do is ignore them. They'll yell and stomp and it may shake you, but don't engage, and when you get home, do some serious self-care. Whatever your favorite thing is, do that. And try your absolute unicorniest to not play the scenario over and over again in your mind. Remind yourself that you already suffered once, and doing

SEE NO EVIL

Don't let evil entities ruin your day or your week or your life. Avoid them if you can. Confront them calmly and honestly if you can't. If you ever feel physically threatened, get out of their way and into a public space as soon as possible. And absolutely avoid that creature in the future.

so again is just another victory for evil. Go to your happy place (page 37) or think about pandas instead (see page 59).

If the evildoer is someone you see on the regular, like a nasty ogre in your group of otherwise lovely friends, let them know you're not weak and they will probably leave you alone. If they insult you, do not attack back, but instead calmly tell them that what they are doing is not OK. Be specific. Instead of saying something general, like "Quit being mean to me," say, "You might not like the way I look, but I do, so stop talking about it." You'll need to mentally prepare for this battle, and it may be that in the moment, they rage out at you. But if you stay calm and hold your ground, pretending you're braver than you are if need be, they likely won't find it worth it to pick on you again.

I LOVE THE SMELL OF GLITTER BOMBS IN THE MORNING

Unicorns live on the high road. That's what makes them so awesome. They are pure cool. But like all rules, there need to be one or two exceptions to prove it. If someone is really under your hide and giving you a hard time, or if somebody really did you dirty, you may perhaps, maybe, possibly somewhat consider a little bit of friendly, totally nonharmful, pretty-dang-funny retribution. Maybe.

If you want to consider this option, you could think about sending a glitter bomb. There are a number of websites that will send one anonymously on your behalf for a little bit of gold. (You can also mail a middle finger, chocolate that looks like poop, or boxes of nothing that are impossible to open.) Or, if you want to smite someone with your own two hoofs, you can make a snarky card, put it crease down into an envelope, pour in a bunch of glitter—the finer it is, the harder it is to clean up—and send it on its merry way.

Also, did you know that you can buy jelly beans in disgusting flavors? That's right! So if you're feeling a little devilish, you might consider dropping off an irresistible sack of candies to your enemy's door. Try a mix of maybe eighty percent gross to twenty percent good if they're not so bright and you think this could get them to keep eating.

IS SOCIAL MEDIA MAGICAL?

You can see pictures of friends and family and artists and celebrities and strangers from all over the world. You can read about ideas from almost any conceivable perspective. You can tap into the entire wealth of knowledge amassed to this point. You can watch a cat wearing a shark costume ride a robot vacuum. That all sounds like magic!

But good magic is often counterbalanced by the dark arts. Pictures you didn't give someone permission to take, let alone share, can be seen by the hordes. You can become the target of harassment and threats. Your identity, money, and credit can be stolen. Pictures of disgusting bodily ailments can pop up when all you did was click on a link for a video of a cat in a shark costume riding a robot vacuum.

Finding your own balance can be hard, but there are a few checks you can put on yourself to make sure you're making the most of the real world as well as the digital realm. When you're in the company of real, live creatures, you really don't need to check your phone very much. If you're paying more attention to posting about your experience than living it, you're missing the magic. If you find your phone is more interesting than the person you're with, it might actually be you who is being boring. (See more on the benefits of limiting screen time on page 41.) Never put more stock in online likes and friend counts than actual friends you like and can count on in the real world.

When you are spending time on social media, make it awesome. Spend time with the stuff that tickles your brain, be it videos of people squishing slime, mixing paint, or applying glittertastic makeup. It doesn't matter what it is as long it's safe and you enjoy it.

Keep in horn, though, that mindless scrolling is bad for the spirit, especially when there is so much out there you can purposefully learn from and delight in. If you find yourself mired in the sargassum of the social-media scroll, try to think of something you've always been curious about and look that up. Ever wonder how glitter is made? Or why we only ever see one side of the moon? Or how planes fly? Or why we drive on the parkway and park in the driveway? All the answers are out there! And if all else fails, or if you just need to be distracted by cuteness, do an image search for "baby animals" and you will never, ever be sorry.

YOUR NEIGHBOR, THE OGRE

The foul smell, the pumping bass, the late-night growling. Your neighbor sucks, and you've had it up to your horn with trying to just ignore them. The question is, what can you do to make things better and not worse?

The answer is weaponized niceness. Being as rude and aggressive as they are will just cause a clash of the titans. Instead, you need to be nice and reasonable and cool—which is your nature, so it shouldn't be hard for you. And it starts before you even have a problem by being a super-cool neighbor who does things like bringing cookies around on holidays and smiling and saying hi, thereby establishing you are cool even if they drool.

If or when problems do crop up, then, you'll be on friendly hoofing already. If they're loud late into the night, one of the most common neighbor complaints, going over and calmly and sweetly asking them to turn it down will go far better for you than screaming out the window at them to shut the elf up. If their piles of bones or moaning maple trees are spilling over your property line, you have every right to clean them up or trim them back, but it might be a good idea to mention it first. A friendly heads-up— "Hey, I'm doing some yard work and just want to let you know I'm cutting back the moaning tree to the property line!"— may make them grumble, but it might prevent a full-on rage that could

happen otherwise. (Such a reaction would be unwarranted and unreasonable, but that doesn't often stop an ogre.)

No matter what the ill is, try to handle it as calmly and in as friendly a way as possible. Your good cheer is your shield and your weapon! Even the angriest ogre will feel ridiculous about getting all riled up in the face of niceness. Usually, anyway. So talk things out as much as you can and try not to escalate to match their bad attitudes. You can always alert the authorities if things get out of hand, but that's probably only going to fuel a feud, so treat it as a last resort.

And know that sometimes you might just have to live with bad behavior that is annoying but technically within the boundaries of "live and let live." Noisy afternoon parties every weekend may annoy you to no end, but some creatures are party animals, and you're not going to be able to change that. A messy yard may not look awesome, but is it worth getting bent out of shape about it?

If you're the one being chastised by a neighbor, really think about whether or not they are being reasonable. Tamping down loud music, even during the day when it's allowed, is considerate even if it is not required. If, however, you're being unduly harassed by a persnickety witch or warlock, get on your grin and arm yourself again with niceness.

THE CHARM OF AN APOLOGY

"I'm sorry" is a powerful magical charm when said sincerely. It can act as a balm to soothe hurt feelings and help wounds heal. For your remorse to be real, it has to come from a place of truly feeling bad for making someone else feel bad. The feeling is about them, not you and your desire to be forgiven.

But sometimes the words aren't enough. Sometimes, if you really screw up, you can make an apology even more powerful by doing something to make amends. Some things are obvious, if not easy to atone for. If you borrow something and lose it or somehow trample it into oblivion, then replace it with something even better than what you borrowed. If you can't replace it right away, a sincere "I'm sorry" that comes with a legitimate replacement plan is in order. (It's a good rule not to borrow things you can't readily replace, as you can end up in some very hot stew.)

If you break a date or a promise, then make up for what you missed by planning an even better date or make doubly good on the benefit of the promise later. For instance, if you promised you'd drive someone to an appointment and then bailed, causing them to take a taxi or miss the appointment altogether, then it's time to play unicorn Ubercorn and offer yourself as a chauffeur service for a certain number of trips.

If you did something really unbecoming of a unicorn, which does happen from time to time no matter how good you try to be, showing how sorry you are can be a challenge. It will have to be tailor-made to fit the crime and to suit the creature you wronged. You're going to have to dig deep and be super sincere as well as patient. How bad you feel and how badly you want forgiveness should be a far second and third to trying to help the creature you hurt heal.

SAYING "I'M SORRY"

An apology should be delivered with genuine feeling. It can come in a card, but that should be followed up by the words themselves said horn to horn and not on the phone or in text.

BE A FORGIVICORN

In life, you will be challenged by many creatures and by yourself. Wrongs will be done to you and by you, purposefully and accidentally. You can get bent out of shape about them, let them ruin your good times, and become a bitter old unicorn, or you can take a deep breath, accept that life is a wild mashup of ups and downs, and forgive. And the unburdening you'll feel is pure magic.

Like many of the really good kinds of magic, forgiving can be hard. It's also kind of nebulous. It's not a perfectly defined thing in the way tangible objects like chocolate and toadstools are. It's something that starts with a bad feeling that you have to transmute into a neutral one. It doesn't mean forgetting an offense entirely, and it doesn't even mean you don't still get a little steamed up when it crosses your mind. What it does mean is that when you think of the offending creature, the bad feelings are not right on the surface; they are not the first things that come into your mind and heart. They may creep in a little, but they aren't as big as the love or warmth you feel. You can get to forgiveness by thinking of all the good things about an offending creature instead of always focusing on the offense. If the hurt was unintentional, really absorb that. Think about the apology given. Even if there was no apology offered or if the offense was a monumental betrayal or mean thing, holding on to bitterness may hurt you more than the offense. Your hurt will

be compounded if you let it live in you for too long. No matter how wronged you were or how justified you are in being angry, at some point you need to let it go, and the sooner you can do that, the better it is for you.

Once you feel forgiveness, you can share it with a simple incantation: "It's all right—I forgive you." Wounds may not totally heal and scars may not disappear just by uttering this, but the poison is gone and the hurt is less hurty, the weight less burdensome. Make sure you actually forgive someone before you say you do. And if sharing your forgiveness may open a door to someone who will only use the opportunity to wrong you more, well, nuts to that jerk! You can forgive them without them ever knowing about it.

Your own self can be the hardest creature to forgive of all, but you have to treat yourself with the same kindness you would treat your best friends and most cherished loved ones. If you did something you would forgive them for, then why wouldn't you forgive yourself? Do what you can to right your wrongs; apologize and make amends. Then forgive yourself. After all, you're only a unicorn, and not even unicorns are perfect.

UNICORN
YOUR HOME

WHEN YOU WALK INTO YOUR HOME, it should feel oh so good. Welcoming and comfortable and perfectly yours. It should be filled with things that make you super happy, with that feel of magic that is so important to the unicorn philosophy. While that feeling itself is a universal unicorn truth, the things that hold that sense of enchantment are different for every single creature. What's right for your home is likely not right for someone else's, and vice versa. You have to hold that sense of you and what you love tight when you're picking out the things for your home. After months of combing through catalogs, the perfect chair may wink at you from a garage sale as you drive by. Or you may fall in love with a giant metalwork equine that makes others raise an eyebrow but that you know is made of pure magic. Keep your eyes and horn open for that glowy aura of meant-for-me, and don't settle for less!

To make an enchanted unicorn home, remember that where you live is where you will go when you're happy and when you're sad, when you're scared and when you're elated, when you're sick and when you're on top of the world. It needs to prop you up and heal you as well as be a podium for triumphs and a sanctuary of fun and wonder! It's where you go to recharge and become your very best self, so treat it with the care it deserves. That doesn't just mean cleaning and organizing—it also means having some fun with it!

This chapter will help you figure out what home goods make you really happy. That special kind of sparkly happy that is food for the unicorn spirit. Objects can hold power, but it's you who gives them that power, so it's important to figure out what deserves your attention and what is actually just clutter that would be better off out of your life. Even if you're a sentimentalicorn, you don't have to keep every scrap of paper that holds a memory.

You'll also learn about the magic of aromatherapy and candles, how to give your bathroom the spa treatment, and the way to construct a truly happy place in your home (and outside it)! There is so much you can do to make your space more magical, and you don't need piles of gold to do it if you are tuned in to you(nicorn) and keep your sense for wonder wide open.

MAKING YOUR HOME FLOW

Have you ever walked into a room that just worked? A space that felt perfectly arranged and felt good to be in? That good energy is magical and can feel quite mystical at that. Figuring out how to arrange things just so may seem a bit mystifying, but the art of feng shui can help. An ancient Chinese philosophy whose name means "wind-water," feng shui is a system for making an environment balanced and harmonious. While the interior-decorating aspect of it is a modern, Western twist, the principles are old, and the results are usually very pleasing.

The guiding principle for harmonizing a home in accordance with feng shui is to make its energy move in a peaceful way, and you can achieve this by placing furniture and objects in ways that will move energy along at a calm pace. You don't want to block energy, which can make you lethargic and sad, but you also don't want it to speed along, as that can make you stressed out and frantic. Imagine that a super-cool dragon of the long, serpentine variety is coming to visit and you want her to be able to move comfortably through your home.

First, there are public spaces and private spaces. Public spaces, like your living room and dining room, can be decorated in energetic, rich colors and should allow energy to flow easily and freely around them. The couch should be set against the wall opposite the doorway, and additional seating should form a circle to facilitate conversation. A circular coffee table in the center with a wide path around it is good—you don't want your dragon guest banging her shins on hard corners. Similarly, the dining room should have a table that balances the space, not so big that the path around it is a tight squeeze and not so small that the room feels like a cave. Placing treasured items where they are the center of attention will make you feel good every time you enter a room.

The kitchen is very important to your health and energy. Ideally, your refrigerator, stove, and sink should form a triangle with an open, easily navigable path between each point. No matter how your kitchen is set up, keeping it well lit, well ventilated, and uncluttered will make for happy cooking.

Private spaces like your bedroom and bathroom should feel inviting and comfortable. In the bedroom, the head of the bed should be as far as it can be from the door, but the feet should not point out the door. Bedding should be luxurious and plush. There should be space on both sides of the bed, and those spaces should have matching lamps to make the room feel balanced. Choose colors that are earthy and natural. If you hang art, it should be happy.

Bathrooms are the hardest rooms to harmonize because energy drains out of them, so it's recommended that you keep the toilet lid down and the bathroom door shut. A mirror will reflect the energy of the room, which is great as long as it's not reflecting the toilet. If you keep the room clean and uncluttered, it can be a sanctuary of purity instead of a drain for your health and wealth.

MINIMALISM VERSUS TCHOTCHKEISM

There are two kinds of unicorns in the world: the minimalist kind, who like an open room with clean lines and just a couple of well-appointed pieces in it, and the tchotchkeist kind, who have an emotional connection to all sorts of baubles and talismans and love to surround themselves with them. OK, well, there are probably a few unicorns in the middle, but you get the drift. Both sides of the spectrum are equally good as long as the way you decorate makes you happy. Your home should delight and enchant you, regardless of what friends, magazines, or relatives say.

The tchotchke-heavy end is bursting with magic. Adorable crystal figurines of rabbits and poodles are delightful, as are tiny toy dinosaurs and miniature landmarks from around the world. They can give your heart a warm hug whenever you see them, but they do also tend to collect dust. If you love something enough to display it, you should love it enough to dust it every now and gain.

In late-medieval Scotland, there were gold coins known as the "unicorn" and the "half unicorn."

Minimalists' hearts swell at the sight of a bright, clean room with perhaps just a single treasure shown off in a place of prominence. Their challenge is that when there are just a few things in a room, they must all work together because each one stands out.

SENTIMENTAL MAGIC

Is it junk, or is it precious? When it comes to a paper plate you turned into a decorative Thanksgiving turkey when you were five, it's hard to tell. Holding on to sentimental stuff can be great, within limits—a favorite teddy bear, a lock of rainbow hair from your first trim. But if you save everything, then by definition, none of it is precious. If you save only the best, then you've truly got a treasure chest.

To determine whether something is junk or precious, ask yourself a few questions. First, is it handmade? A card from a

distant or departed loved one that's heartfelt and handmade can be precious while a generic card with just a signature scribbled in it may well be junk, especially depending on the answer to the next question . . .

How many similar items do you have? If you have just one card from a particular person, it's worth saving. If you have a card from this person from every holiday of every year since you were born, well, you might not need them all. It's similar with your paper-plate turkey. Saving one super-cute thing you made as a kid is sweetly sentimental, while saving boxes of them dilutes the specialness of each one.

Even if you've determined that something deserves the junk pile, letting go can be hard. Just thinking about getting rid of it can make you feel like you're throwing away love. In those cases, have a little parting ceremony. Spend a moment with each item to appreciate it, take a picture of it (digital of course), and then say goodbye. If a garbage bag seems too sad an end for it, place it gently in a box that you can close the lid on and get rid of.

CRYSTAL POWER!

Bringing crystals into your home is a great way to make a space feel really good and look really enchanting. Different crystals and stones are said to have different properties, and you can use them to summon the good vibes you're looking for.

Amethyst is calming. It brings contentment and can help you meditate and destress. By putting an amethyst crystal in each of the four major corners of your home, you can ward off the heebie-jeebies.

Citrine brings success and abundance. Putting one under your pillow can scare away nightmares.

Pyrite helps with focus and emotional well-being. It also stimulates creativity and willpower.

Clear quartz is energizing and amplifies positive energies. This one is a true classic!

Rose quartz fosters love and chases away negativity.

Tigereye grounds you and helps you grow your wealth through awareness and understanding.

Celestine is balancing and opens up lines of communication. It can also help you remember your dreams.

THE ENCHANTED ART OF DECLUTTERING

Sentimental objects and tchotchkes aside, there is plenty of stuff that can fall into the clutter category. The longer you live in a home, the more likely it is that you've got stuff stuck all over the place that you really don't need. Maybe you have an entire cupboard stuffed with plastic shopping bags that you plan on reusing but seldom do. Perhaps you have some broken items you've been meaning to fix for far too long, or any other odds or ends that you've had plans to repurpose for so long but never get to. The time may have come to say goodbye to yesterjunk.

Start with spots in your home that feel like they're bursting. Take every single item out of the bursting closet, drawer, container, or wherever. Clean out the space itself and then take a hard look at each thing. Do you actually use it? If the answer is yes, it's obviously a keeper. A hard no answer is equally obvious—toss it! If the answer is that you want to use it but don't, put it aside. Anything that falls into this good-intentions pile can go in a storage box. If you don't open the box for six months, take it out but don't open it. Can you remember what's inside? If not, just get rid of the whole thing! If you do remember some of the stuff, take it out and put it somewhere where it's in your way for two weeks. If you still haven't done anything with it by then, it has to go!

Clothes follow a similar rule. Go through your closet and drawers, sorting things into piles of what you wear all the time, what you wear occasionally, what you intend to wear but don't, and what doesn't even fit anymore. The first and last categories

are easy: things you wear all the time get put away and things that don't fit get tossed or donated. It doesn't matter if you have every intention of fitting into them again one day. (OK, OK, you can save one absolutely favorite item that you want to fit in again someday. Just one, though!)

Things you wear occasionally can be kept, especially if they are special-occasion clothes and that's why wearing them is rare. If you wear something but you actually hate it and feel off when you wear it, just get rid of it. There's no reason to keep its bad mojo hanging around. And if you have things that you mean to wear but never ever do, give yourself two weeks to wear them. If you still haven't put on that crocheted glitter top in that time, out it goes!

A PLACE FOR EVERYTHING AND EVERYTHING IN ITS PLACE, DAGNABIT!

The most magical thing you can do for your home is to have a place for everything. If all your stuff is organized and living in designated hidey-holes, meaning you're not jamming odds and ends into places where they'll languish forever forgotten and unused, well then you are not only a unicorn—you're a wizard!

Here are a few tips on how you can graduate from the Homewarts School of Organizational Wizardry.

Shelves, bins, and organizers are amazing when used well. If you don't have a specific place where you keep something, it's bound to become clutter, so having thoughtfully designed places to store your stuff is essential, 101-level stuff. Look at the things that you leave lying around a lot. If they don't have good homes, get or make them for those items. Maybe you have a problem with the mail always being left around. Get a hanging organizer that separates mail into bills, letters, miscellaneous keepers. Only allow mail to live there, and toss everything that doesn't fit into one of those categories as soon as it comes in.

Things you use all the time need to be easy to get to and easy to put away or you'll just leave them out. If you're a crafty sort of unicorn, this means having containers or even a rehabbed suitcase partitioned in a way to hold the tools of your trade. Stuff you only use occasionally can be tucked away up high.

For batteries, gift-wrapping stuff, fancy napkins, extra wires, and all the other doodads you do use but not often, the trick is to keep them out of sight but well labeled. Storage drawers in a closet that are easy to get to and have a contents list on the front are nothing short of magic. If you can't identify something, that means it's garbage.

If your kitchen drawers are overflowing with utensils and your cabinets are an avalanche of pots and pans, do a purge of the stuff you don't use and then do yourself a favor and get some organizers. Hanging pots and pans is a great way to make them accessible without worrying about them crashing down on you.

Don't overstuff any room or any space. Jamming too much in leads to losing things, getting frustrated, and living with a mess that irritates the heck out of you. Keep what you use and nix what you don't (see page 144 for tips on decluttering).

The final exam is the hardest bit. Organizing systems work only if you use them. Just having the drawer dividers and adorably labeled containers in place won't save you if you don't take the time to put things where they belong. If you don't put something away, it's something out of place, and the more things that are out of place, the more cluttered your space and the harder it is to get back to that magical realm of sorted serenity. So take the extra second to put something away when you use it and save your sanity down the line.

HOME OF WONDERS

Central to the unicorn way of life is a focus on the little magical bits. The things that make you happy and give you a sense of enchantment. The things that sparkle and wink and seem to give off their own radiance, even if that beauty is only in the eye of one beholder. Here are some ideas for things you can do to create moments of wonder around your home:

Diorama Drawer Now that you're so well organized, you may have a drawer or two to spare. In it, you can create a top-view diorama of an enchanted forest or a secret garden known only to you. In it you can put some of your most precious tiny things.

Plants Most Unusual There is nothing like a little greenery to keep a home happy and fresh, but what about a little pinkery or purplery? There is a wide world of unusual plants you can keep, from purple clover to Red Velvet echeveria to fuchsia itself. There are also some amazingly shaped plants, such as *Crassula umbella*, dolphin succulents, and zig-zag cacti.

Fairy Doors If you have a tree you particularly love, you can add a little door to the base of its trunk. This lets fairies know they are welcome, and you can leave them gifts and notes behind the door. You can either buy or make a fairy door, and how you attach it to your tree can be anything from working hinges to just propping it in place with some stones.

SECRET SPOTS

False-bottom drawers, boxes disguised as books, loose floorboards—is there anything more enchanting than having a secret place in your home where you can squirrel away some treasures?

BRINGING THE RAINBOW INSIDE

Unicorns have a pretty distinctive color palette: all the colors! The whole rainbow tends to be unicorns' favorite color, which means an exciting world of opportunities as well as a challenge. While you may want all the colors to be present and accounted for, making them work in harmony without being overpowering takes some thoughtfulness.

Start by giving each room or space its own theme. Walls painted in a neutral base color, like warm off-white, make a beautiful showcase for an accent wall in a bright color and art and décor that abide by the magic of color theory. Color theory takes the rainbow and matches up the colors that work well together. If two hues are opposite each other on the wheel, they are complementary and work together. Blue says to orange, "Hey, good looking," and orange says, "Back at ya!" So if you have a blue accent wall, orange décor will pop nicely against it.

Analogous colors are friendly neighbors on the wheel. Putting reds, oranges, and yellows together makes for friendly relations and a pleasing ombré. Triadic colors are matched by tracing a triangle between three points on the wheel. These form bold contrasts that are tricky to make work in a single space, but it can be done if you have a good eye.

KEEP THINGS FRESH

Change is not just inevitable, it's wonderful, and it's something you can embrace in your home. While you don't have to repaint with the seasons or rearrange the furniture annually, a refreshed room does have a magic all its own.

You can freshen things up simply by keeping flowers. Bringing in some fresh cuts every week keeps things moving and seasonal. There will always be something new and lovely to catch the eye.

Getting cases for your throw pillows and rotating them out every few months will keep your pillows looking and smelling fresh. You can buy these cases from lots of home-décor places, but squares are super easy to sew, and making things yourself adds a charm no store-bought item can create.

Vinyl wall decals and temporary wallpaper are fantastic ways to change up the look of a room. Easy to put up and even easier to take down (with no damage to the wall), they are kind of magical. There are thousands of patterns and images out there, and you can even create your own designs.

Moving around your art and décor is another easy way to make a room look new again. You don't have to replace what you've got in there, but if you rearrange it, it'll catch your eye all over again and renew your appreciation for an old piece.

FOREVER PIECES

Just because you want to keep a room fresh doesn't mean you shouldn't invest in some staples that you plan to have for a long, long time if you're in a place you're going to live in for a long, long time. Getting well-made furniture fashioned from real wood and other quality materials is worth the money. Things made with care feel better to be around, and if a curio cabinet makes your heart sing or a claw-foot library table sings to you, it's better to spend some money on something that sparks your heart and that you'll have for a long time than to keep buying cheap stuff you have to frequently replace.

While forever pieces can be costly, they don't have to utterly break the bank if you go antique and take your time. You can find marvelous things if you keep your mind and imagination open to the possibilities of refinishing a beat-up bookcase or reupholstering a chair that looks a little homely but is the most comfy thing you've ever sat in. Unicorns are not afraid of putting in a little elbow grease when they spot an enchanting buffet table hidden under layers of dust and dirty doilies.

FLAT-PACK TRICKS

If you're not in your forever home or if you just like to keep your furniture current, flat-pack build-it-yourself pieces can have their own magic. You can hack, modify, paint, and plunder them to suit whatever need you may have. One trick is to use some fancy hardware to make something like a dresser go from flat-pack obvious to obviously fancy.

You can also feel good about using your own artistry to customize furniture you didn't pay a ton for. While you may not want to paint swirly vines onto a walnut cabinet, you should have no such compunction about going to town on a set of thirty-dollar shelves. Washi tape, paint, stencils, carving, and even markers can be used to personalize any piece you like.

Dipping spindle legs in paint is a great way to pump up the wow factor on an otherwise uninspired piece. And making multiple surfaces multiple colors—wood grain for the sides of a dresser and white for the drawer faces, for instance—adds distinction and unicorn class.

Don't feel confined to the intended purposes of a piece. You can change out the legs of a table to make an ordinary desk into an out*standing* one. Use some wire legs to make an otherwise plain side table into a statement piece. If you find some lovely tea towels, you can make them into kitchen curtains with some simple stitches or even just a few clothespins. Putting some wheels on a side table can make it into a bar cart in no time. It just takes a little time, a little creativity, and maybe some Internet searching.

YOUR HAPPIEST PLACE

Every unicorn home needs one spot dedicated to happiness—a spot you can go to that feels so comfy and magical and joyful that you smile just thinking about it. This is the place you can go to meditate (see page 31) or practice visualization (see page 35) or read a book or calm down or recharge or generally just feel really good. It doesn't have to be big or lavish, but it has to be yours and spark that feeling of magic.

The requirements to make your happy place feel magical are basic. You need to be able to sit comfortably there. A comfy chair is great for most of your happiest place's purposes, but if you meditate, you should also have a little spot of rug to sit on. From where you sit, you should be able to gaze at something that makes you happy. A window that looks out onto trees (but has a shade or curtain you can draw) or a tapestry or abstract piece of art that makes you feel calm and happy can all work, but you do you! Though you may be spending a lot of time with your eyes closed while in your happiest place, it should delight you when you have your eyes open.

Around you should be some things that you love. This is the place to showcase and spend time with the objects that feel most magical to you. The objects that hold a sense of wonder and love—a cherished tchotchke, a memento from a loved one, an heirloom from a beloved family member. You also want

to make the spot charming and inviting. A vase of flowers you regularly refresh, your dream board, and crystals (see page 143) are all lovely options.

Lighting is a fun consideration. You don't want bare bulbs shining in your eyes; instead, soft, warm light that infuses the spot with a glow is good. A Himalayan salt lamp (see page 163) is a wonderful choice. If you have a window in your space, sheers that let the light glow instead of shine in beams are lovely.

Infusing the room with aromatherapy is a great final touch for creating the mood you're looking for (see page 165). You can do this with candles or one of the many varieties of diffusers.

Though you should have at least one happy place in your home, that doesn't mean you should have *only* one. If you have the room, why not make a few? A dedicated reading nook, a perfectly decorated desk where you craft and write, a comfy nook in the kitchen where you fantasize about recipes. You can make magic anywhere inside! And an outdoor happy place, where you can plant so many enchanting flowers or sit in the shade of a majestic tree, is a wondrous thing too.

ALLURING LIGHTING

The way you light up your life is an ambient and all-important element of comfy happiness. If you are always squinting in low light to see when reading or crafting, turning your head to avert your eyes from harsh brightness, or fumbling around to even turn a light on, you should consider working a little magic on your lighting situation.

You should easily be able to flip a switch to see as soon as you enter a room. If you have to bumble across the room in the dark, consider putting a little lamp closer to the entryway. Rewiring in the walls can be a pain well worth enduring (and shelling out some gold for), but you can also affix a corded "lamp to the wall near your doorway. Just make sure it's got an easy mechanism to turn it on. You can also get a clapper device that just requires you clack your hoofs together to turn lights on and off, which is a pretty dang enchanting way to make anything happen.

Different rooms call for different lights. Consider first where you most often are in a room. You don't want lights shining into your eyes while you're sitting on the couch or lying in bed. Consider diffusing glass globes to surround bulbs for these situations, or place lights behind where your head will be. Reading and standing lamps are great to have so the light can be bright when you need it and soft when you don't.

The dining room is the perfect spot for an elaborate light that gets to be the center of attention. A beautiful crystal chandelier or stained-glass hanging lamp makes a wonderfully enchanting focal point, and there are so many designs out there that you should be able to find one that feels perfectly magic and exactly made for you. The kitchen needs bright lights to illuminate what you're doing. A light over the sink and stovetop in particular make kitchen tasks all the easier.

Once you have the perfect fixtures for your rooms, picking appropriate bulbs is the all-important finishing touch. There are so many choices today, which can be overwhelming but also means that with a little consideration you can always have exactly what you want. Incandescent bulbs are the classic kind and typically give off a warm light in glass that ranges from clear to all the colors of the rainbow. When you're looking for a certain vibe and don't need to see particularly well, colored bulbs can really change a room. Halogen bulbs look like sunlight and will make the colors in a room sharp and true. Fluorescent tube lights are often very bright but cold lights, though if you look, you can get these in different colors or put them on dimmers. If you have a large area to light up, they're a good choice. Fluorescent bulbs (or compact fluorescents, aka CFLs) are energy efficient, don't buzz as much as their big brothers, and come in a range of warmths and brightnesses. LED lights are the best at efficiency and come in a super-wide range of colors.

BEATING THE SADS

Feeling SAD (seasonal affective disorder)? Then you need blue and white lights! These simulate the sunlight you miss in the winter.

THE ANCIENT MYSTICAL PROPERTIES OF HIMALAYAN SALT LAMPS

You'd probably think that if you can get it at Bed Bath and Beyond, it can't be full of ancient magic, but you, my gorgeous unicorn friend, would be wrong. Pink Himalayan salt is available in many everyday stores, and it's not just ancient but prehistoric, as it was formed over 250 million years ago from marine fossils in a long-dried-up seabed. Today it's mined from a few areas around the Himalayas, and it gets its warm, pink hue from some mineral impurities (more like mineral beauties!).

You can of course eat this tasty salt like you would any other, but using a large piece as a lamp or candle holder is an awesome additional use for this sodium-chloride wonder. First off, it is said to clean the air by giving off negative ions, which can counteract harmful positive ions given off by heat and electronics and life. Negative ions increase oxygen to the brain, which increases alertness and combats the drowsies.

They've also been promoted as ways to help with allergies, decrease coughing, reduce static in the air, help you sleep better, and treat seasonal affective disorder. Granted, that's a tall order for a little chunk of mineral, but even if none of that is true, what is undeniable is that the soft, pink, glowy light is truly enchanting. And everyone looks their best in soft, rosy lighting. If it looks like magic and feels like magic, it must be magic!

THE SPELL OF THE FLAME

All the elements are enchanting, but fire may be the most entrancing. The glow it gives to a room is warm and conjures up an inborn sense of wonder that is singular to the flame. If you have a fireplace, use it. You may make excuses not to light it because of the care it requires, but an evening on the hearth gazing into the flames holds a spell of relaxation, magic, and recharging that is unmatched by anything else.

An outdoor fire pit is a simple alternative to a fireplace. You can find them in a great many stores in a great many shapes and sizes. Just picture yourself under the stars, watching the dancing flames and maybe roasting a marshmallow or two. What a magical night!

Candles are lovely little pieces of wonder, too. They come in so many colors and scents, and they each can protect the life of a single flame. A candlelit room conjures peace and romance, taking you out of the modern age with all its flashing lights and into a serene cocoon that feels like the rooms that unicorns lived in so many centuries past.

AROMATHERAPY: SMELL THE MAGIC

Filling your space with lovely scents makes for a beguiling multisensory environment. Different scents can help create the mood and energy you're looking for and can even ease headaches and sinus issues for some. The first thing to do is to decide how to get the scent out there.

Scented candles and incense are among the more ancient techniques for infusing a space with a smell. If you go for these fire-based practices, be sure to get a trusted, natural brand. You don't want to burn anything but the best natural ingredients, and you certainly don't want to be setting harmful chemicals alight.

If you're going with essential oils, you have a number of options for diffusers. The classic way to use this type of scent magic is with heat diffusers, which often look like lovely little ceramic toadstool houses with inverted caps. In the bottom sits a tea-light candle, which, when lit, heats the dish above, where the oil sits. Once the oil warms, its scent disperses into the room (though some believe the heat neutralizes the magical properties).

Nebulizers use pressurized air to turn essential oils into a fine mist that floats through the room. Ultrasonic diffusers emit frequencies that vibrate water to the point of vaporization. The water then lifts up through the essential oils and carries it around the room. These methods don't require heat and are recommended by oil experts.

Once you've picked your method of scent delivery, you can pick the scents themselves. You can find oils at lots of home-goods stores as well as in enchanting shops dedicated to crystals, scents, and magic. If you're looking to just make a room smell nice, follow your nose and pick the oil that makes you feel best when you smell it. Or you can think about what you'd like the scent to do and choose your oil that way.

For calm, destressing, and sleep: lavender, chamomile, geranium, rose, bergamot, sandalwood

To ease sorrow: frankincense, patchouli, jasmine, sandalwood

To reduce anger: rose, jasmine, chamomile, patchouli

To soothe headaches: lavender, eucalyptus, peppermint, rosemary

To open up sinuses: thyme, eucalyptus, peppermint, rosemary, tea tree

For romance: rose, jasmine, vanilla, sandalwood

For energy and happiness: lemon, orange, jasmine, cinnamon, peppermint

Blending scents is a lovely way to personalize your experience. As you get more familiar with the different smells, you'll likely come up with your own concoctions to make you feel your best. A drop of this, two drops of that, a dash of the other, and voilà— you have your own signature happy scent!

MAGIC MESSAGES

It's a very old tradition to leave incantations around the home to spark inspiration and love and to pick you up when you're feeling down in the horn. A cross-stitched reminder that home is where the heart and horn are, a pillow proclaiming "bless this mess," a poem engraved on a piece of wood—these have graced abodes for centuries, and today you can find them in abundance. You can get a sign that says anything you want, whether predesigned or of your own making. You can hang it proudly near the entrance to let visitors know yours is a house filled with life, laughter, love, and if they don't like it, they can get the elf out!

While these messages are often meant to be seen by visitors, they are words that feel like magic to you, that resonate with you. And you don't always have to put them out there for anyone to see; you can leave messages just for yourself or your loved ones. Inside the bathroom mirror is a great place to put a list of guiding principles, as you're likely to look there every morning. On days that you know will be hard, it can be a real pick-me-up to be reminded that you are loved and that you act always with that love in mind. A piece of paper in a drawer that simply has a smile drawn on it is bound to make you smile back.

home is
where the
heart and
horn are

TRANSMUTING A BATHROOM INTO A SPA ROOM

A steamy shower, a hot bath—these simple luxuries do wonders for the spirit. Upping your spa game in the bathroom can be excellently easy with amazing results. You can start by decluttering surfaces. A simple basket, standing set of drawers, and, if you're short on space, a cabinet that goes over the back of the toilet are great ways to get your beauty tools out of sight when not in use. Soothing, clean colors and art can boost your bathroom's sense of calm. The natural light of a window is wonderful for a bathroom, but if you don't have one, pick lighting that emulates daylight and diffuses it to every corner when you want it and dims to soothing darker shades when you don't.

A deep tub is a thing of wonder. There's nothing quite so soothing as sinking down into a hot bath. A bubble bath is a classic spell for luxuriating and relaxing, but other enchantments come in the form of sparkling, fizzing bath bombs. You can turn your bathwater into a perfumed kaleidoscope of colors and glitters that soothe your haunches and delight your nose while the effervescent bubbles tickle your bottom. Flower petals are another charming way to make bathwater more magical. Now add some candles and a warm, wet compress over your eyes—

The famous medieval *Unicorn Tapestries* series depicts a unicorn purifying water flowing from a fountain.

perhaps with a drop of your favorite essential oil infused into it—and you'll find yourself in unicorn heaven!

But you don't need a bath to have a spa experience in your bathroom. Showerheads come in an amazing array of spray options, and they can be as easy to install as screwing on a new head. You can emulate the pitter-patter of rain or the downpour of a waterfall. Many heads come with a variety of settings so that you can tailor each shower to your mood. Shower wands often have this feature with the added bonus of mobility.

If you want to go the extra mile in bathroom luxury, a towel warmer is a modern enchantment you really should consider. You can get either warming drawers or racks that make your towels toasty and warm. You can also put warming elements into the floor itself so that your hoofs stay nice and cozy even on cold mornings. And while we're on the subject of warming, you can also get a heated toilet seat to toast your buns!

Speaking of the commode, your European and Asian unicorn sisters know all about the wonders of a bidet. They're a bit foreign to American sensibilities, but think on this: if you got dirt on your hoofs, would you be content to just wipe them off with paper, or would you want to give them a rinse? Mm-hmm. That's what I thought. Bidets do just that for your tush, and you can get them with warm-water options.

A UNICORN'S PANTRY

Keeping your favorite food on hand is a great way to make magic moments in your day. Really savoring something is a delight you can have daily, so why not do it? When you go to chow down on your next snack or meal, really take it in before you feast. The smell, the feel, the color. If it's homemade, think of the love that went into making it. The charm of cherishing your food just can't be beat.

Exploring new foods is a wondrous and winsome activity. Here are some enchanting items you might consider adding to your pantry:

- ♥ Fairy Tale eggplant
- ♥ Chocolate Stripes tomatoes
- ♥ Polar Bear pumpkins
- ♥ Cinderella pumpkins
- ♥ Golden Jubilee peaches
- ♥ Cotton Candy grapes
- ♥ King Arthur peppers
- ♥ Ambrosia apples
- ♥ grains of paradise
- ♥ Red Bliss potatoes
- ♥ Black Lava salt
- ♥ Eclipse cheese
- ♥ treacle
- ♥ mooncakes
- ♥ ribbon candy

RAINBOW CAKE!

Want to make the most magical of all the cakes? Then you have to put a rainbow in it!

Cake Ingredients & Tools

2 boxes white or vanilla cake mix

eggs, oil, butter, and whatever else is called for by your cake mix

red, orange, yellow, green, blue, and purple gel food coloring

3 eight-inch round cake pans

1 big ol' bowl

6 small bowls

measuring stuff

cooling racks

cooking spray (optional)

Butterlicious-cream Frosting Ingredients & Tools

1 cup (.5 liter) vegetable shortening

1 cup (2 standard sticks, 330 grams) butter, softened

2 pounds (1 standard bag, 32 ounces) powdered sugar

2 teaspoons vanilla

3 to 4 tablespoons (45 to 60 milliliters) whole milk

1 big ol' bowl

electric handheld mixer

frosting spatula or regular spatula

Bake That Cake!

1. Preheat your oven to a toasty 350°F (175°C).
2. Grease your cake pans with butter or cooking spray.
3. In the big ol' bowl, mix all the cake ingredients together except for the food coloring.
4. Divvy up the batter evenly between your 6 small bowls, putting about 1⅓ cups of batter into each.
5. Use the food coloring to dye each bowl to your desired saturation. Start with a little coloring and keep adding to get to the perfect color. Remember: you can add color, but you can't subtract it.
6. Pour 3 of your colored batters into your 3 pans and refrigerate your other 3. (If you have more pans and an enormous oven, you can bake as many as you like at a time.)
7. Bake the 3 pans of batter for about 18 to 20 minutes, until you have a springy cake that bounces back from your touch and just starts to pull away from the sides of the tin. Let them cool for 10 minutes and then remove them oh so carefully from the pans and let them cool completely on the racks.
8. Wash your pans and repeat the baking and cooling process. Admire the colors! You're such a cool unicorn.

Icing Magic!

1. In your big ol' bowl, beat the shortening and butter together with the mixer on medium speed until the mixture turns a cheerful light yellow.

2. Downshift to low speed and slowly beat in the powdered sugar. Next comes the vanilla.

3. Then add in the milk, 1 tablespoon at a time, until your yummy frosting is nice and smooth. Then put your pedal to the metal! Beat your frosting on high until it becomes light and fluffy like a cloud.

Make Your Rainbow!

1. Now comes the delicate work of stacking your cake layers. If any are a little uneven on top, feel free to give them a careful trim.
2. On a pretty cake plate, put down your purple layer and spread some frosting around on top of it, but not quite to the edge.
3. Place the blue layer on top and continue in reverse rainbow order.
4. When your rainbow is stacked and frosted together, ice the outside into one big puffy cloud!
5. Marvel at what a dang fine baker you are.

RAINBOW SWIRL

If you don't want to fuss with layers, you can make a rainbow swirl! In rainbow order, starting with red, drop some batter into your cake pan, then add the next color to the center of your first dollop of batter. Your cake batters will spread out slowly to make concentric rings of color. You can use all of a color at once, or you can make lots of swirly layers by going through the rainbow a few times.

ENCHANTED GARDEN

Planting seeds, saplings, or any other baby plant and watching them grow into glorious nature is spellbinding. The things you can grow are endless and can be perfectly suited to your climes and tastes. There are easy gardens of wildflowers, vegetable gardens of sustenance, and complex gardens of neatly manicured foliage. Whatever your tastes, don't be shy about adding some extra-magic elements, including the fairy doors from page 149.

Birdbaths and birdhouses invite your avian friends to come and play at your house. You can also put up feeders if you want to give them a feast. Using specific seeds and feeder types can attract certain feathered friends, such as hummingbirds.

Fountains are a soothing way to add a little water and movement to your garden. Their gurgling babble is truly enchanting, and you can get fountains that light up the water flows with rainbow colors!

Wind chimes will sing to you as you tend your garden, and they make really lovely visual additions as well.

A secret spot in a dense patch of tall grass or flowers makes a truly bewitching hideaway where you can enjoy some secluded peace amongst no one but the buzzing bees. If you want some extra company, there is no shortage of magical creatures you can get in the form of statuary that you can put in your secret spot or throughout your yard. And even if a trinket wasn't specifically designed for the outdoors, if it seems weatherproof, why not tuck some toy dinosaurs or other beasts wrought in plastic in little corners and crannies of your yard? So long as what you use is out of the path of the mower, why not tickle your fancy with all manner of innovative yard décor?

A BUTTERFLY BUSH

While there are countless numbers of flowering shrubs, vines, and trees, a unicorn's yard is incomplete without a butterfly bush. If you live anywhere but the coldest of places, you can grow the *Buddleia davidii*. Most commonly it has big conical sprigs of purple flowers that last all summer if you tend them. The *Buddleia marrubiifolia*, or wooly butterfly bush, does better where it's hotter. Its flowers are big and orange and beautiful!

A butterfly bush does well in full sun, and it will flower and flower and flower as long as the weather is warm and you cut away spent flowers. The abundant nectar of the flowers will attract a truly amazing number of butterflies, as well as bees and hummingbirds, who will all will bring your yard to life with iridescent fluttering wings and zealous buzzing.

UNICORN
YOUR JOB

A JOB CAN BE FUN AND FULFILLING, making all your sparkletastic dreams come true while also making you fabulously wealthy. Or, perhaps more often, it can be one of the most decidedly un-unicorn parts of your life and do none of those things. Instead of running wild and free, being majestic and magical as you are truly meant to be, you *have* to go somewhere, no matter how much you don't feel like going. Even when the sun is shining and the birds are chirping and the flowers are blooming and beckoning you to frolic with them, you have to show up to a place where you probably didn't even get a say in the décor. Maybe this place has no windows, the fluorescent lighting buzzes infernally, and there are repetitive swathes of gray carpet, walls, and clothing.

Who knows what dark magic decided gray and repetitive was a great way to design a place where people spend the majority of their waking lives most days of the week? Thankfully, with a little bit of unicornification, you can break that spell or any other version of it that may afflict the place where you spend your working hours, be that an office, a school, a restaurant, or anywhere else on a unicorn's sparkly earth. You just need to tune in to your unicorn vision so you can spot the glitter and pops of magic in even the most dismal of environs and coax those bits into bloom.

Worse than bad decorating is the fact that you don't often get a say in what creatures you work with. The world is populated with all manner of trolls and ogres, but don't forget that there are also many fairies and elves, phoenixes and fellow unicorns, and other companionable creatures who may be hiding their enchantments under dowdy sweaters or stuffy suits. You just need to know how to soothe the beastly cohorts into docility, or at least non-nuisance status, and then how to catch the kind of sparkle in people's eyes that betrays an enchanted creature within.

Worst of all, though, is if you don't like what you do every dang day. That can be the worst. *Can*, though, does not mean *has to*. There are many ways in which a bad job can dull the golden sheen of even the brightest horns, but there are ways to glitter-bomb even the wickedest bosses, toughest jobs, and ugliest spaces into something you don't just live with but thrive in. Sometimes this means spotting little glints of magic and shining them to full luster, and other times it means creating your own magic throughout the day.

WHAT KIND OF MAGIC SHOULD YOU MAKE?

No matter what your job situation is—whether you're looking for your first one, trying to find a new one, or content to keep on doing what you're doing—every now and again, it's a good idea to evaluate your skills, your ambitions, and what the heck you want to be doing. Make sure you're on the right path through the forest, so to speak. This aptitude quiz is designed with your inner unicorn in mind, so take it to find out what makes that pretty horn shine.

1. How much do you love talking to strangers?
   a So much! Give me all the strangers!
   b It's pretty good. I usually enjoy a random chat.
   c Eh, I could take it or leave it.
   d I don't love it, but I do it when I have to.
   e Literally, it's my worst nightmare.

2. How much do you love math, data, and crunchable, black-and-white facts?
   a So much! Give me all the numbers!
   b They're pretty good. I usually enjoy a spreadsheet.
   c Eh, I could take them or leave it.
   d I don't love them, but I use them when I have to.
   e Literally, they are my worst nightmare.

3. How much do you love telling people what to do?
   a So much! You will all obey me!
   b It's pretty good. I usually enjoy running the show.
   c Eh, I could take it or leave it.
   d I don't love it, but I do it when I have to.
   e Literally, it's my worst nightmare.

4. How much do you love being on your feet, moving around, and generally not sitting still?
   a So much! I *need* to keep moving!
   b It's pretty good. I usually enjoy being active.
   c Eh, I could sit or I could stand.
   d I don't love it, but I do it when I have to.
   e Literally, it's my worst nightmare.

5. How much do you love helping people?
   a So much! Do you need something? I'll be right there!
   b It's pretty good. I usually enjoy helping out.
   c Eh, I could take it or leave it.
   d I don't love it, but I do it when I have to.
   e Literally, it's my worst nightmare.

6. How much do you love being left alone?
   a So much! Solitude is my fortress!
   b It's pretty good. I usually enjoy alone time.
   c Eh, I could take it or leave it.
   d I don't love it, but I do it when I have to.
   e Literally, it's my worst nightmare.

7. How much do you love making things?
   a So much! It's all I ever want to do!
   b It's pretty good. I usually enjoy making things.
   c Eh, I could take it or leave it.
   d I don't love it, but I do it when I have to.
   e Literally, it's my worst nightmare.

8. How much do you love breaking a sweat?
   a So much! Get me moving!
   b It's pretty good. I usually enjoy working it.
   c Eh, I could take it or leave it.
   d I don't love it, but I do it when I have to.
   e Literally, it's my worst nightmare.

9. How much do you love feeling needed?
   a So much! I need you to need me!
   b It's pretty good. I usually enjoy feeling useful.
   c Eh, I could take it or leave it.
   d I don't love it, but I live up to my obligations.
   e Literally, it's my worst nightmare.

10. How much do you love starting a project from scratch?
    a So much! Give me that blank canvas!
    b It's pretty good. I usually enjoy the challenge.
    c Eh, I could take it or leave it.
    d I don't love it, but I do it when I have to.
    e Literally, it's my worst nightmare.

WHAT'S YOUR CALLING?

If you answered *a* or *b* on 1 and 3, you're a **public relations wizard**. Not in the sense that you *have* to do PR specifically, but in that you're good at talking to people and getting them motivated to do great things, so you'd rock a job that has you interacting with the public or lots of different people. This could be retail, sales, marketing, event planning, fortune-telling, or anything else that lets you get out there and impress folks with your majestic self!

If you answered *a* or *b* on 2 and 6, you're a **lone werewolf**, a fierce genius when allowed to be independent and just get plop done. You take a problem and crush it with your fearsome jaws of intellect, and you don't need anyone to tell you how it gets done. This makes you perfect for being a programmer, editor, analyst, cat burglar, land surveyor, or hermit with a claim on a riverbed that's all atwinkle with gold.

If you answered *a* or *b* on 4 and 8, you're a **busy bee body**—literally, a body that likes to be busy. It's a good thing! Honest. You're someone who has to be on the move and on your feet.

To you, a desk is death, and if you're not sweating you're not living! You'd make a killer fitness instructor, pro athlete, restaurant server, construction worker, landscaper, farmer, professional wrestler, forest ranger, or treasure hunter. Something that keeps you moving will keep you happy.

If you answered *a* or *b* on 5 and 9, you're a **helping hero**. You are happiest when you're coming to the rescue, supplying succor, aiding the injured, and fighting the good fight. You are a do-gooder, and that's great! The world needs more yous. And it's good for the rest of us that you being the awesome aide that you are makes your day. If you can make your money having your day made, then you've got it made. Savvy? You'd make a phenomenal doctor, social worker, counselor, white witch, customer-service rep, or masked superhero.

If you answered *a* or *b* on 7 or 10, you're a **magic maker**. You have a creative genius that cannot and should not be suppressed. You see a blank piece of paper, a lump of clay, or a jar of glitter and you have a million ideas on how to make a million things out of each of them. Inspiration pops and bangs in your brain, and you love it! Take that creative power and become an awesome artist, writer, chef, graphic designer, circus performer, landscape architect, or fashion designer for celebrity pets.

If you didn't answer *a* or *b* on any questions, you're special indeed.

DEALING WITH DISASTER DAYS

Some days are just the worst. No matter how good you are—and dang, you are good—the trolls and ogres and dark forces of the world sometimes conspire to rain down doom and gloom. Or sometimes you screw up; it happens to every single living thing, even unicorns. When everything goes wrong, all you can do is run damage control and then take super-awesome care of yourself.

First, don't beat yourself up. That's the most important thing. You're only a unicorn, and even unicorns aren't perfect. Instead of worrying yourself sick over what went wrong, focus on fixing it and learning from it. Bosses are impressed not only with how employees do things right but also by how they handle the pegasus plop hitting the fan. So don't waste energy going down the dark path in the forest of elf-ups. Instead, focus on cleaning up the mess and moving forward. Be honest, be proactive, and don't dwell on dookie.

Then treat yourself. Do something you love. Watch your favorite movie, have your favorite meal, make sure you see the sunset, partake in some retail therapy, go running if that's your thing. Do whatever it is that makes you happy, and remember that there is just so much more to this big, blue world than your mistake.

Lastly, plan a future treat. Think of something you really want to do, something you've been meaning to do for a long time and just haven't yet. Then make a plan to actually do it. Research the heck out of it. Get a crew together to do it with you. Take a nice long time being utterly distracted from the disaster by planning something great and wholly unrelated to it.

CONJURING A COOL COMMUTE

Getting to and from work can be obnoxious, perilous, repetitive, and downright infuriating. But you can cut down on the awful with the right attitude and accessories. Like most things, commuting is made worse by focusing on how sucky it is. And while you might not be able to totally block out the fact that you're jammed onto a train or stuck on a road full of ogres who somehow managed to get cars, you can depressurize the suckiness by bringing a thermos of your favorite morning bevvy. And don't just suck it down while grumbling—sip it. Savor it. Focus on how lovely and warm and amazing it is.

A playlist for every occasion is great to have at hand. Create one to get you pumped, one to mellow you out, one that is straight-up Fun Town USA, and one to work out your aggression. Audiobooks that take your mind well off the roads and tracks of your everyday commute are also magical AF.

If you drive to work, deck out your car in all manner of cuteness. Dangly crystals, little figurines on the dash, a plush steering-wheel cover. Those beaded seat cushions are no-joke comfort. Anything that makes you smile when it catches your eye (but doesn't distract you from the road, obv) or puts you more at ease will help lighten the load of driving the same path every day.

Speaking of that, if you can manage to build a little extra time in, try taking different routes to work. If there are some back

roads that take you ten minutes out of your way but through some gorgeous trees or rolling hills, it's worth the extra traipsing.

If you're a public-transportation-icorn, there's nothing like a movie or episode timed to match your commute to make the time fly. On the bus or train for forty-five minutes? Break out your tablet or phone, pop in those headphones, and be on the train in body but out of the train in spirit.

For those of you who get crammed into vehicles of transport more like sardines than the mystical beings you are, it can be really hard to find some peace, let alone some magic, especially when others are behaving badly—blocking doors, man(ticore) spreading, eating smelly mutton, whatever. When you can't even move your arms to read your book or look at your phone, all you can do is creature-watch. Marvel at all the kinds of beasts and beauties there are. How there are billions of lives being lived billions of ways, but you're all doing this one, wild, ultramodern thing together. It's an amazing time to be alive, even when you're just riding the train to work.

THE MOST MAGICAL JOBS

There are some really amazing, unicorntastic jobs out there. Maybe not a lot of people get to do them, but *some* people get to do them, and you're some people—heck, you're *better* than some people—so why not you?

Horologist Someone who studies time, the measurement of time, and clocks. There are few things as enchanting as the intricate workings of clocks. The gears, the chimes, the solemn marking of the world passing by. It's really a very magical art, and you could be the tinkerer who gets these things ticking!

Ice-Cream Taster Yes, this really is a job. It helps to have a degree in food science to get the gig, but there are legitimate companies out there that will pay you to taste ice cream and judge it. Taste, texture, hidden treasure veins of marshmallow. These things can be your purview. Did I mention they *pay* you to do this?!

Hot-Air-Balloon Pilot Imagine it. You, an old-timey hat, and maybe a pocket watch or other steampunk accoutrement to help you really feel the part as you conduct a basket attached to a giant rainbow balloon through the puffy clouds and singing birds of the sky. You have become a unipegasus!

Magician If you *really* wa
magical job, then you can
always go full bore towar
your dreams and become
a magician. This is
someone who *does*
magic. Magic is their
entire thing. It's kind
of all they do. You can
say phhhh, they're just
tricks—they're not really
magic. But what's more
magical than making
folks happy as you
procure bunnies from
hats and flowers from
thin air? No matter how
it's done, that's magic.

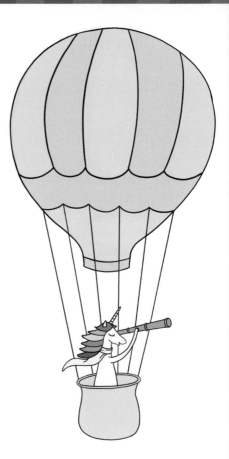

FINDING MAGIC ON THE JOB

No matter what your job is—apothecary, actuary, or trapeze artist—some days just feel like you're scraping your way up some godforsaken mountain in Mordor. They don't call it the grind for nothing! The key to getting through the day with a smile on your face, or at least without wanting to tell everyone you hope they end up on the wrong end of your horn, is to find one small thing about it that makes you smile. That's the whole unicorn philosophy! Find that one sparkly bit of magic in something, and home in on it. Bring it to the forefront. Focus your energy on it. Embrace the shimmer! Make it your happy place, moment, thing, whatever, that you can go back to or call up and get a smile from it. And once you have one of those sparkly bits—just one—keep it safe and find another. Then another. Then another, until you have so many magic moments going that they easily counterbalance the nonmagical junk moments.

Finding shimmery enchanting bits at work can be tough. Real tough. But they are there! And they aren't necessarily job related. Start with things near your job that you can focus on while you're on your way to work instead of just dreading the heck out of your day. Maybe you go by an adorable dog park where the little woofers play, and you get a giggle out of it. Or there's a coffee shop with the best rainbow latte you've ever slurped. Think about those when you're going to the grind.

When you get there, hold the happiness of those things tight. Bring them in with you. Then you'll likely have an easier time finding some magic at your actual job. Do you have a work friend who's the coolest or the cutest or both? Make sure you get in a morning laugh with them. Take the way that laugh feels with you to the less magical parts of your day.

When it comes down to the work itself, well, it's all about the story you tell yourself. If you dread it and hate it and grumble about it like a troll with a thorn in your toe, then it will suck. No doubt about that. But if you don't tell yourself a bad story about it over and over again and instead find just one little thing you like about it—how fast time goes when you're really focused, the sense of accomplishment you get at the end of something, how good it feels to get something right, or even just the cute font you use in your e-mail—and sink your teeth into that, it'll all get easier. I swear on all that is rainbow and bright that it's true. If you stop telling yourself you dread something, even when you do dread it, and instead tell yourself the stories you like, that dread will melt away like bitter winter frost in the spring sunshine. If you feel the dread coming, think about those dogs in the park or that friend or how good you are at what you do and just dig in. Hold on to the magic; let go of the muck.

MAKING MAGIC MOMENTS AT WORK

When you're unicorning your life, a lot of the time you have to make your own magic. This is especially true at work. Embracing the bright spots that are already there is certainly important, but creating your own is even better. You'll find lots of ways to make your days brighter throughout this chapter, but for now we'll focus on setting up a few magic moments you can go to each day. Because, for the love of leprechauns, you deserve a fiver every now and then. Give your eyes, hoofs, or whatever a rest. You'll also be surprised how much easier it is to solve a problem or finish a job once you clear your mind for a hot minute.

Make your breaks twinkle by:

Taking fantasy breaks! Have an audiobook queued up that will whisk you somewhere far away for a few minutes. Somewhere enchanting and beautiful, dark and mysterious, or breathtaking and thrilling. There's nothing quite as transportive as having someone tell you a good story.

Going outside! It really does a creature good to get out in the air and under the big sky, so go on—go through that door. Walk around the block. Watch the clouds. Find a pretty spot and take a mini mind vacation (see page 37).

Taking a bewitching beverage break! Everyone trudges over to the break room to get a coffee or tea when they need a pick-me-up, but yours is going to be special! Turn making it into a ritual. Make it perfect. Make it delicious. If your job doesn't provide deliciousness, bring it from home. And don't take your magical brew back to whatever it was you were doing. Take the time to savor it and get recharged.

Having an afternoon dance! You probably go from powerful unicorn to lethargic sloth about three-quarters of the way through your day—still cute, but not fast moving. It's the nature of work, but it doesn't have to get you down. Find a private place (you might have to combine this with the "going outside" tip), bring your headphones, and have a one-unicorn dance party to your favorite track. If you've got some cool party beasts at work, make it a joint venture.

Calling your BUF (Best Unicorn Friend)! Make a five-minute phone call (in private—your coworkers don't want, need, or deserve to hear it) to your favorite friend and tell some jokes, gossip, make a fun plan, talk about anything positive and non–work related (i.e., don't talk about work!).

DIY UNICORN FRAPPA-YUMMO

The Starbucks Unicorn Frappuccino. It was sweet, it was sour, it was lovely. It also came and quickly went. RIP, SUF. Luckily, it's not that hard to make an equally beautiful and delicious version of this drink yourself so you can keep your unicorn levels powered up to the ultimate anytime you like.

Frappa-Yummo Ingredients & Tools

½ cup (120 milliliters) ice

¾ cup (175 milliliters) milk

2 scoops vanilla ice cream

½ tablespoon mango syrup
(Torani brand
if available)

1 tablespoon Kool-Aid Pink
Lemonade unsweetened
drink mix

½ tablespoon grenadine syrup

blender

measuring stuff

Sour Syrup Ingredients & Tools

½ teaspoon Kool-Aid Blue
Raspberry Lemonade
unsweetened drink mix

½ teaspoon hot water

¼ cup (60 milliliters) white
chocolate, melted

small mixing bowl

whisk

Toppings

whipped cream

more of each flavor of Kool-Aid

Unicorn It!

1. Blend all your Frappa-yummo ingredients together until smooth and awesome. If you want to pump up the pink, add more grenadine.
2. Whisk together the Blue Raspberry Lemonade mix and the hot water. Slowly mix in the melty, gooey, yummy white chocolate until everything is mixed together and lovely. If it's too thick or hardens at all, add just 1 drop of water at a time until you get a pourable syrup.
3. Get a big old glass, preferably a clear one so you can see the unicorny colors. Fill it about a third of the way with your Frappa-yummo and then drizzle your syrup along the inside surface of the cup and into the drink itself. Give it some time to slide down the sides. Then pour in the rest of the Frappa-yummo and top with as much whipped cream as you can manage. Dust it with a bit more of your two types of Kool-Aid powder.

SPRINKLE, SPARKLE, SCRUMPTIOUS

There are lots of delicious ways to unicorn your noms and bevvies. Rainbow sprinkles are a classic! (Unicorns call them sprinkles, not jimmies. "Jimmies" is just wrong.) You can also get edible pearl dust and metallic mists. Food coloring now comes in all the colors of the neon and pastel rainbows, and if you want to go natural, beets make great pinks and radicchio can be sweetened up for blue.

BAG OF TRICKS

Life (and work) is just a lot more wonderful when you're prepared—and not just for the bad. Sure, it's good to be braced for when evil mojo comes your way, but it's even better if you've got the supplies to make some magic happen whenever you want. So keep a supply kit at work that will have you ready for anything and everything, from a sour stomach to surprise party. Here are some things to keep in your bag of tricks:

- ♥ aspirin or another analgesic
- ♥ chocolate
- ♥ glitter
- ♥ zit coverup
- ♥ zit cream
- ♥ tampons and/or pads
- ♥ hairbrush
- ♥ scratch-off lottery ticket
- ♥ tiny, adorable toy
- ♥ yo-yo
- ♥ whistle
- ♥ moist towelettes
- ♥ deodorant
- ♥ dry shampoo
- ♥ amazing lipstick
- ♥ comfy shoes
- ♥ badass high heels
- ♥ nail file
- ♥ needle and thread
- ♥ stockings
- ♥ stain stick
- ♥ spare shirt
- ♥ spare underwear
- ♥ squishy stress ball
- ♥ bouncy ball
- ♥ horn polish

- ♥ lollipops
- ♥ bag of chips
- ♥ magazine
- ♥ flashlight
- ♥ phone charger
- ♥ markers
- ♥ all sorts of stomach medicines
- ♥ allergy medicine
- ♥ tissues
- ♥ Rubik's Cube or other puzzle
- ♥ one of those keychains in the shape of an animal that, when you squeeze, poop pops out, but obviously one in the shape of a unicorn that has sparkly poop—yes, of course these exist and can be easily found and purchased online

CREATURE COMFORT

You've gotta be comfy if you want to be worky. If you're on your feet a lot, this means shoes that feel as good as they look. Maybe better. (Probably better.) Don't ruin yourself by jamming your hoofs into killer shoes day in and day out. Find pairs that sparkle and make you happy but that don't jam your toes, make your back ache, or neglect your arches.

If you're a desk jockey, make friends with the mystical art of ergonomics. There are lots of handy calculators online that will tell you how tall your chair, desk, and screen should be for your height. Your hoofs should be flat on the floor, but the average desk is twenty-nine inches high, which is too tall even if you're six feet tall. While you can't shrink your desk, you can get a box to put your feet on. Standing desks are rad and keep your shanks in shape, and sit-stand desks are the best of both worlds.

A good chair at the right height can save you lots of pain in the future. You want your elbows to bend at ninety degrees, and you want the back of the chair to support your lumbar area. A lumbar pillow can turn an average sitting experience into one of ergonomic perfection. A trackball mouse is easier on the wrist than a regular mouse, and a squishy pad in front of your keyboard is like a dreamy pillow for your joints. Even though sitting all day doesn't seem taxing, it's hard on the body, so make sure you treat your beautiful self right.

UNICORN TEARS ARE MAGIC

No—really! Tears have the power to cleanse and heal. After a good cry, that's precisely what has happened. You feel like you've shed a little bit of the burden or hurt or stress. Crying is absolutely nothing to be ashamed of, even when it happens at work, which it does to most unicorns at least once. Some creatures rage and stomp and yell, and that's how they deal when things go wrong for them. Unicorns are much more decorous and gentle beings than that, so tough times bring out a much gentler response. Some fools may say this is a show of weakness, but they are likely the same trolls who think a stomping-and-yelling tantrum is a sign of strength. Crying displays a deep care and regard for your work. You're investing not just your time and energy but your emotions as well. Just because you're a pro doesn't mean you're a robot. You've got feelings and passion, and when they bring you to tears, you can cry with dignity.

If it's only a little misting up or a tear or two, just dab your eyes, keep your head high, and do *not* apologize. If you're still composed even though your eyes are a little rainy, then staying strong and proud through it will impress. If it's going to be a real thunderstorm, excuse yourself from the room, find a private place, and let it all out. When you return, again, don't apologize. If some dope thinks crying is a weakness, an apology will reinforce that bad idea. Don't give that satisfaction.

THE OFFICE OGRE

Every workplace has an ogre. Or two. Or thirty. They grump around the office, or whatever your place of work is, and complain about the boss, the pay, the coworkers, the coffee, the lighting, the temperature, the dying ficus in the lobby, the anything and the everything. And while there's no denying that a little commiseration can build camaraderie, do you ever feel *good* after talking to them? Maybe you feel like you've blown off a little steam, but do you feel positive and full of majesty, as you should? Or do you mostly feel drained and a little bit to a lotta bit angry? These are certainly not very sparkly things to feel, but that's what the office ogre feeds on.

An ogre is someone who is angry at the world. They don't see rainbows and roses; they see rain clouds and rot. They walk around just waiting to be insulted or irritated so that they can point it out and be mad at it. So, basically, they're the opposite of unicorns, who are always on the lookout for the good in everything.

Office ogres can be tricky to deal with because it's easy to end up on their dump-on list if you don't play their ogre games and agree with all their grump. That's not necessarily the worst thing in the world, but it's not fun either. To stay on the good side of an ogre without succumbing to their gloomy moods, you can smile and nod at their stories without taking them seriously and then offer them candy. Perhaps a giant gobstopper to stop up

their giant gob. You can leave cake in the kitchen and, when they come by, say, "Did you hear there's cake in the kitchen? I already had some, but you should go get a slice before it's gone." If the ogre doesn't have a sweet tooth, you can change the subject to something you know they like. Cats or sports or something.

Whatever you do, do not tell the ogre to cheer up or give them direct advice. This is anathema to them, and they will stomp around and get even grumpier. You can, however, tell them your own stories and how they resolved happily. So instead of saying, "You know, Bob, you should really just water the ficus if it bothers you so dang much," say, "I had a ficus at home that was dying—turns out I just wasn't watering it enough!" They won't ever take this not-advice, but they will notice that you use your unicorn judo to flip all their negative Nancying to positive Pollying, and they'll eventually lose interest in complaining at you without getting outright annoyed and putting you on the dump-on list. The key here: don't let their negativity dull your shine. Stay sweet, stay positive, tune them out if they don't shut up, and don't let the inevitable ogres bring you down.

MAGICAL HEALTH DAYS

They say mental health days, we say magical health days. Ours are better, but no matter what anyone calls them, these days are not just important; they're obligatory. That's right, as of right now, you absolutely *have* to take them when you need them. There will always be a hundred reasons not to take a day off when you really need it, but remember how important you are. Your being healthy and great and balanced and happy is the greatest goal you have, so do what's needed to make that happen. And that means taking a day off (if possible) even during the busy season.

So when the stress is getting to you, or the weather is amazing, or you've had it up to the horn, or you just really need it, take it. Take the day and do something *amazing*! You could:

- ♥ ride a roller coaster
- ♥ go for a hike
- ♥ build something
- ♥ paint something
- ♥ play something
- ♥ sew something
- ♥ brew something
- ♥ write something

- ♥ go for a long drive
- ♥ go to a petting zoo
- ♥ adopt a kitten
- ♥ go fruit picking
- ♥ go to the beach
- ♥ go to the desert
- ♥ go to the mountains
- ♥ take a super-long bath

- 💜 get a mani-hoofi
- 💜 scream into the void
- 💜 play with friends
- 💜 rearrange your furniture
- 💜 do some yoga
- 💜 sit in on a lecture
- 💜 dance your face off
- 💜 go on a date
- 💜 hang out with your mom
- 💜 go shopping
- 💜 drive an hour to eat something amazing
- 💜 sleep
- 💜 do a puzzle
- 💜 read a book
- 💜 plant something
- 💜 arrange some flowers
- 💜 go to a museum
- 💜 go to two museums
- 💜 see some sports
- 💜 test-drive a sports car
- 💜 knit
- 💜 sing at the top of your lungs
- 💜 go for a boat ride
- 💜 do whatever touristy thing there is to do near your house
- 💜 ride a bike
- 💜 ride a horse
- 💜 ride a merry-go-round
- 💜 meditate
- 💜 start a fire (in a fire pit or fireplace, of course!)
- 💜 squish some slime

DEALING WITH THE HORDES

If your job has you interacting with the teeming hordes, i.e., the public, then you likely get a really wide range of experiences, from delightful to icky to downright devilish. You never know whether the person you're about to talk to will reveal themselves to be a fellow unicorn or a foul creature from some sulfurous swamp. When you get the latter, you will have to treat them like they're rational and totally normalsauce when they are in fact saltier than potato chips—angry, angry potato chips. So how does one keep one's cool?

When you come up against the irrationally irked, the unreasonably uppity, the bafflingly belligerent, and the enragingly entitled, there are a few things you can remember that will keep you from banging your horn against the wall. First, they have to be them. Forever. They have to be that creature who feels those foul feelings all the time. They have to live with themselves, which is a pretty bad punishment, while you get to be you, which is pretty amazing! At the end of the day, they'll be snarling over nonsense, and you'll be giggling over glitter, so you win. A lot!

Second, don't expect them to be anything but themselves. They are not calm. They do not make sense. And you can't change that. Being exasperated at their absurdity over thinking they deserve something or trying to understand why they think you did something to offend them when you were being super cool is just a waste of your own precious energy. You'll never pull them up into the lovely land of logic, so just try to figure out what will make them be quiet and go away, and focus on that. If they feel slighted, tell them you're sorry they feel that way. If they think your place of work owes them something, do your best to give them that thing or some token that will appease them if it's no shine off your horn to do so. If you get riled because they're riled because their brains are made of rocks, then they've won. If you remain calm, feel sorry that they don't get to be a unicorn, and help them as best you can by figuring out what kind of creature they are, then you win—and they even win a little, which they might really need. Remember, they always have to be them, and maybe that should earn them at least a little sympathy.

CREDIT VAMPIRES

These foul creatures lurk in the shadows, waiting to steal the credit for the hard work of others. They may be your coworker or even your boss. No matter where they rank, they *are* rank. And it can be really hard to figure out how to make sure your own work gets noticed when they are trying to suck out all the glory for themselves. No one wants to come across as a braggart or a tattletale. It can not only be difficult but also feel inappropriate to say, "Oh, Linda didn't do that awesome job—I did!" So what do you do so you still feel unicorneriffic and appreciated?

First, deep breath. Don't do anything when you're angry. That's a pretty good rule for most situations, and it super applies here. Then consider that the credit vampire may not know what they're doing or that they're doing it. It might be their natural defense mechanism when they feel scared. This doesn't excuse the behavior, but it will help you not feel so bent about it. Also consider whether an event really matters. Will it hurt your career, your chances for a raise or a promotion, your reputation? If the answer is no, then let it slide, but put your guard up to make sure that you're extra careful to attach your name to any work that the credit vampire might try to feast on in the future. If you work with this creature on projects, decide when you start one how the work and the credit will be addressed. Keep a record of it and refer to it at the end. If they

somehow manage to suck all the credit down, break out that record and ask them to right the wrong.

If the credit vamping has any chance of hurting you, your rep, or your future, then you've gotta do what you've gotta do. You can start by talking to the credit vampire, saying you know it was likely an oversight, but you worked hard, and it would be great if they could follow up with the team to let them know what part you worked on. If they aren't outright evil, they will likely feel like they have to fess up. If they *are* outright evil and won't share credit even when asked (or you know asking is futile), then you will have to chime and toot that old horn of yours yourself. If possible, do this in a private conversation with your boss. If not, then you can couch your own accomplishments in a synopsis of the project in which you outline all the parts you accomplished. This may be in a meeting or an e-mail chain. Just chime in with, "A lot of work went into making this happen. When I . . ." and tell the facts just as they are. The truth is not a brag.

WHEN YOUR BOSS IS A BEAST

Some bosses are forged in fiery pits of molten suck by dark wizards of toil and trouble. It can seem like the only thing they actually do is plot out how to steal your magical thunder and make your life as miserable as possible. You're fairly certain they've got a doll in your likeness that they push pins into and twist in all sorts of uncomfortable, taxing positions. Or maybe they're just horribly inept. They might just be absolutely crap at managing people, or perhaps they don't care about you or their work or anything except extreme workouts and protein smoothies. Whatever their beastly downfalls may be, it's up to you to not let them get you down.

First, figure out what makes them happy and do that. What kind of things do they seem to value? Punctuality? Good

grammar? Hitting deadlines? If the answer feels like "absolutely nothing," or if it feels like they have a grudge against you specifically, then you may have to make a counterintuitive leap or two. Do your best to try to make them look their best. Compliment them in front of others. Ask them questions about their weekend or personal life. Treat them the way you'd like to be treated. At the very least, you'll be doing the right things. You'll be acting the way one should act, and that's often the best you can do. Don't let a bad boss drag you down to the depths. Keep right on shining, and people will notice.

If you're dealing with a bully, then stand up to them. Don't cower and let them overpower you. Be cool, be strong, be you! You don't get stepped on or dragged down. If they're yelling, tell them that you are happy to discuss the issue but you would appreciate being spoken to with respect. If they're pushing blame on to you, be straightforward in telling them that you need them to set the record straight. It seems daunting, and maybe even impossible, but tough beasts need this kind of confrontation. It's all they understand.

And if it all just gets to be too much and you're thinking of taking your magical powers elsewhere, consider going to HR or even your boss before you make the final decision to hit the road. If you're good at your job, odds are that even if you're being mistreated, you are in fact valued. Air your grievances, because you don't have much to lose if you're thinking of quitting anyway. Be honest, be cool, and be prepared with specifics. You will likely be very surprised by the response you get.

MEETING MAGIC

☆ ☆ ☆ ☆

One of the most common complaints people have about work is there are just too many dang meetings. Launch meetings, status meetings, recap meetings, meetings to talk about the problem of too many meetings. And while there is usually a valuable moment or two in every meeting—some vital info passed along, some gossip about that irksome ogre traded—there is a lot of time you have to spend looking bright eyed and bushy maned while people talk about stuff that has next to nothing to do with you. It's tempting to spend that time on your phone, getting actual work done or perhaps looking at those hypnotic slime vids on Insta, but that's kinda rude and will win you exactly zero brownie points.

Instead, bring a notebook. That way you can work on your to-do list, draft some e-mails old-school style, or, best of all, play Buzzword Bingo! All you need to do to play is come up with a list of the insufferable jargon people in your meetings always use

BRING A FRAPPA-YUMMO

Keeping caffeinated during snoozy meetings helps you stay awake, and the sipping gives you something to do every time you feel your horn start to droop. (See recipe on page 203.)

and either make a bingo-style grid of the words or tick off how many times someone says each one. You can have a subversive chuckle to yourself while actually still paying attention to what people are saying. Win-win. Or at least not lose-snooze.

MIXING WORK AND PUFFY HEARTS

Getting a work crush is almost inevitable. You spend a lot of time with your coworkers, and some of them are darn cute! The roguish elf, the saucy sphinx, and even the wily wolf all hold their own brand of allure. Having a sparkly dreamboat at your job can make your day a little lighter and a lot more fun as you hope to spot them at the watering hole or the copy machine. It's when things get real that the cool waters of a fun flirtation can become the rapids of a monster disaster.

Hooking up might seem like an awesome idea after happy hour, but you are going to see that person tomorrow. And the next day. And the next. And so on. It's hard to keep things casual if someone has hopes or expectations that go beyond a smooch fest. So if you're going to do it, try to make sure you're both thinking the same thing.

If you *are* both thinking the same thing and that thing is "Let's make an awesome couple and date!," be sure you've considered that you will see each other every ding-dong day.

Normally you wouldn't see someone so much when you start dating, because that's a recipe for a short-lived disaster. Plus, it takes away from the mystery and excitement of a new relationship.

But when that someone is your coworker, you have no choice but to see them super frequently. Even if you're fighting. Even if you're in a bad mood. Even if you don't feel like putting on your best face. Even if you're thinking of breaking up with them. Even if they're thinking of breaking up with you.

That's not to say finding an awesome partner at work is always a forbidden-fruit situation (though it is if that fruit is your boss or if your employer has policies against coworkers dating). But you should exercise a good amount of caution before running horn first into something with someone you're feeling shaky about. Try to stretch out the just-friends period for as long as you can stand it. Be open and honest about your feels and your likes, but hold off on the forging of relationship bonds until you're pretty dang certain you want to be shackled to your honey-to-be.

HOME-OFFICE HEAVEN

Working from your home, most likely in your PJs, is a dream come true for a lot of unicorns. For others, it can get kind of lonely or boring or distracting or unfulfilling or all of those things. Whether you're living your dream or feeling alone in the void, there are a few things you can do to make the most of your work-from-home hours.

You definitely need a dedicated space. It might not be a full room, but it should at least be a place that is totally devoted to work stuff. Set it up so you're not staring at temptations like your soft and dreamy bed, inviting couch, or super-entertaining TV. Also, make it a place you want to be. If it's an ugly mess, you might find yourself avoiding it like a troll bridge, but keeping it organized and cute makes it easier to hunker down.

It also helps if you can quarantine the space, so it's separated off from your luxurious living areas with a room-dividing screen or some other visual barrier. Not only will this help you concentrate and feel like you're truly "at work" during biz hours, but it will help you physically and mentally partition off the work part of your day from the homey part of your day. You don't ever want to stop being able to tell whether you're working from home or living at work.

CONSUMING WITH CRITTER COHORTS

Happy hour is one of the best bonding experiences you can have with your fellow beasts. Corporations spend all this money on team-building exercise programs, but the real getting-to-know-each-other happens quite naturally and often magnificently at the bar after the workday is done. Ogres, trolls, sphinxes, wolves, unicorns, elves, manticores, pegasi, mummies, and more can all find something in common over elixirs and brews.

Most of the time, these are some of the best times you'll have with your coworkers. But then, of course, there's always someone who takes it too far, gets too honest, makes the hour a little too happy. Don't be one of those people—that's all there is to it. Have fun, be a sport, partake, imbibe, let your hair down, even shake your haunches, but keep it under control. If you're wondering whether one more is one too many, it is. If you aren't sure if you should do something, you shouldn't. If you know that once you get on the party bus you will always take it too far, then order a club soda with lime and it will look like a vodka tonic. Just be cool and casual. Have fun, and remember that tomorrow you still need these merrymakers to take you seriously.

A BIGGER POT OF GOLD

You've been getting the same amount of gold for a year or maybe even more. Each day, you do the most unicorneriffic job you can do—well, most days, anyway. You know it's time your efforts get recognized with a few more gold nuggets in your pot, so how do you get your boss to part with a little more treasure?

First, schedule a time to talk. Don't just casually prance on over and blurt out, "More gold now!" And definitely don't ask in an e-mail. Set up a meeting and prepare for it. Schedule it after a big accomplishment, or, if your job has performance reviews, that's another good time to do it. Don't do it when your boss is spitting fire from stress.

Some people find having the give-me-more-gold conversation hard, but remember: you don't show up all the time because you like it there. You may very well like it there, but at the bottom, it's business, and you deserve to be compensated for your time! Bring a list to the meeting of all the things you've kicked tail at as well as a summary of responsibilities you have now that you didn't have the last time you discussed gold-nugget allotment. The convo should focus on why you *deserve* more nuggets, and definitely not why you *need* more nuggets. Your personal money needs are irrelevant to your boss, so don't bring them up. And don't mention inflation. Your boss knows about inflation. And don't bring up coworkers' pots of gold. Though there is change

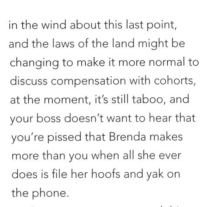

in the wind about this last point, and the laws of the land might be changing to make it more normal to discuss compensation with cohorts, at the moment, it's still taboo, and your boss doesn't want to hear that you're pissed that Brenda makes more than you when all she ever does is file her hoofs and yak on the phone.

In case you get a no, and this can happen no matter how magical of an employee you are, be prepared for that. Ask whether the nugget withholding is due to budget or your performance. If it's the former, ask for a timeline of when you can expect your nuggets to come through. See if there are some other perks you can get in the meantime. Maybe work from home one day a week or get some more vacation time to come your way. If it's the latter, ask what you can do to get more nuggets in six months. Recap that to-do list in an e-mail, do the things on the list, and in six months have your meeting again.

HOLD YOUR HORN HIGH

One of the toughest parts of doing anything for eight hours a day (or more) is staying straight doing it. I'm talking posture here. Sitting and staring and clicking and clacking can be murder on your normally regal bearing. Let's go top down to make sure you're keeping your horn held high and in the right position.

Screens have a tendency to draw us in, to pull us forward to look at them. Remember to keep your ears in line with your shoulders. Speaking of shoulders, pull those beauties back, open up your chest, breathe deeply, and give that magnificent heart room to thump. Get a lumbar pillow to keep your lower back in place and out of pain (see page 208). Uncross your legs, and keep those tootsies flat on the floor or on your foot support. This can be hard to maintain, as we squirm and fidget naturally throughout the day, but crossing your legs or sitting on your feet

GOOD POSTURE, GOOD MOOD

Slouching makes you feel like a slouch! Seriously, science says so.[5] Sitting and standing straight, on the other hand, can improve that mood and make you more confident.

will strain and strain and strain those lovely legs and everything they're connected to.

If your job keeps you on your feet, the same rules apply for head and shoulders. Your back should be straight, not bowing in or rolling. Your tummy should be tucked in a little, which will bring your tailbone forward ever so slightly. This will tighten the heck out of your core. Knees should be straight but not locked, and feet should be about shoulder width apart. Balance your weight as evenly as you can between your heels and the balls of your feet, and keep your feet pointing outward just a teensy bit.

DÉCOR YOU ADORE

If you've got a dedicated workspace, make sure you decorate it to make it yours. The better you feel in your space, the better everything will be. While you don't want to go over the top and set off a glitter bomb, you can bring in tasteful touches for that magic spark that's so important to the unicorn philosophy.

Lighting is crucial, and fluorescents are the worst. If that's what lights up your workplace, bring in your own dang lamp; if you can't turn off the fluorescents, you can at least combat them with a warm, glowy light like a Himalayan salt lamp (see page 163).

If tchotchkes are your thing, bring 'em! A few little frog figurines, some small succulents, maybe some glittery butterflies—as long as they don't dominate your desk but add private little moments of magic, they can really help you get through your day.

Pictures of loved ones and your happy places in the world are, of course, always good to have around. If you've got two monitors, run a video of a waterfall on one if you're not actively using it. A dream board of stuff you'd really like to buy with the gold they're paying you can serve as much-needed reminders of why you're there when the going gets icky.

POWER POSE!!!

You've got a big meeting coming up in ten minutes. Maybe a big presentation. Maybe it's in front of all the giants at your work. It's tense. There's a lot riding on it. You've got your best, most amazing power outfit on, your mane is looking amazing, and you're so prepared it's not even funny. You've got this! But you've also got a bad case of the nerves. Your horn is starting to sweat, and maybe you even feel like you could poop a rainbow. Have no fear! Power posing is here!

Power poses are stances you can strike to get your energy going. Literally. Holding yourself high can make you feel more confident. There have been some claims that this is science, but really, it's magic.

Before your meeting, find a place you can be alone and stand with your feet shoulder width apart and your arms up in the air in a giant V for victory! Take some deep breaths. Feel the power! When you're in the meeting, stand tall, shoulders back, hoofs on hips or spread out on the table in front of you. Make some eye contact. Take up space! Have an open posture. Don't slump, cross your limbs, lower your horn, or look down or away.

Remember, everyone feels the nerves before a big something; it's how your amazing brain interprets those nerves that makes the difference. Many actors feel stage fright, but they find it exhilarating. It makes them want to kick rump! So when your pulse quickens and your hoofs start to sweat and you're feeling that ancient fight-or-flight impulse, remember you're a unicorn and you're going to use those feelings to be awesome!

ENDNOTES

[1] Matthew Thorpe, PD, PhD. "12 Science-Based Benefits of Meditation." HealthLine.com.

[2] Tori Rodriguez. "3 Easy Visualization Techniques." RealSimple.com.

[3] "How Corporations Changed Our Brains." *The Leonard Lopate Show*. September 11, 2017.

[4] Thai Nguyn. "10 Surprising Benefits You'll Get From Keeping a Journal." HuffingtonPost.com.

[5] Lindsay Holmes. "6 Reasons Good Posture Can Make Your Whole Day Better." HuffingtonPost.com.

ABOUT THE AUTHOR

Mary Flannery is a writer and editor living in the New York City area with her husband and two fish. Studying philosophy in college showed her that the mind is an amazing thing, and people can believe just about anything under the right circumstances. Also, the Stoics were really onto something by accepting that the world is the way the world is and the only thing you can control is your reaction to it. She is less on board with the self-denial bit, but hey, pobody's nerfect. Her current philosophy is that magic really is everywhere if you are willing to believe in it—even on the subway if you're willing to believe extra-super-mega hard.

ABOUT THE ILLUSTRATOR

Drue Wagner is a freelance illustrator and graphic designer. She got her start at Pentagram Design in Austin, Texas, then dove into the magazine world in New York City, working for various publications including *GQ*, *Bon Appétit*, and the *Wall Street Journal*. She now lives in Austin again and is enjoying the switch to more illustration work, eating breakfast tacos, and swimming at Barton Springs Pool.